KU-178-058

THE BOY WHO FELL FROM THE SKY

50 Greek Myths

Lucy Coats read Ancient History at Edinburgh University, then worked in children's publishing and now writes full-time. She is a gifted children's poet and has written several picture book texts. Anthony Lewis is a well-known illustrator and his picture books have sold in many countries.

Also by Lucy Coats

Atticus the Storyteller's 100 Greek Myths

Coll the Storyteller's Tales of Enchantment

The Wooden Horse

50 GREEK MYTHS

LUCY COATS

Illustrated by Anthony Lewis

Orion
Children's Books

This edition first published in Great Britain in 2005
by Orion Children's Books
a division of the Orion Publishing Group Ltd
Orion House
5 Upper St Martin's Lane
London WC2H 9EA

An Hachette Livre UK Company

3 5 7 9 10 8 6 4

The stories in this volume were originally published as part of
Atticus the Storyteller's 100 Greek Myths, first published by
Orion Children's Books in 2002

Text copyright © Lucy Coats 2002
Illustrations copyright © Anthony Lewis 2002

The right of Lucy Coats and Anthony Lewis to be identified as the
author and illustrator respectively of this work has been asserted.

All rights reserved. No part of this publication may be reproduced,
stored in a retrieval system, or transmitted, in any form or by any means,
electronic, mechanical, photocopying, recording or otherwise, without
the prior permission of Orion Children's Books.

The Orion Publishing Group's policy is to use papers that
are natural, renewable and recyclable products and
made from wood grown in sustainable forests. The logging
and manufacturing processes are expected to conform to
the environmental regulations of the country of origin.

A catalogue record for this book is
available from the British Library

Printed in Great Britain by
Clays Ltd, St Ives plc

ISBN 978 1 84255 145 5

For Mum, with love.
LC

For Mo, Paul, Francesca
and Lawrence.
Wherever you may wander . . .
AL

CONTENTS

~ 1 ~

FATHER SKY AND MOTHER EARTH

In the time before time began there was only Gaia, the beautiful Earth, and her husband Uranus, the Sky. Uranus loved Gaia so much that he wrapped his great black cloak of twinkling stars about her, and danced her all around the heavens. Soon they had twelve beautiful children called the Titans, who became the first gods and goddesses. But then lovely Gaia gave birth to more children, and they were not beautiful at all. Uranus hated the ugly one-eyed Cyclopes babies as soon as he saw them, and when he was shown the hideous hundred-armed monsters that came next, he roared with rage, and locked them all up in the dreadful land of Tartarus, which lay deep in the depths of the Underworld.

Gaia was very angry, because she loved all her children whatever they looked like, and she vowed to punish Uranus. She gave a magic stone sickle to Cronus, her youngest son, and sent him to fight his powerful father. Cronus was dreadfully frightened, but he loved his mother, and always obeyed her. So he hid in a fold of his father's cloak, and waited till Uranus was not looking. Then Cronus gave Uranus such a great wound with the sickle that Uranus fled into the furthest part of the heavens and never returned.

Then Gaia married Pontus the Sea, who covered her body with his beautiful rainbow waters, and as a sign of her love for him, she gave birth to the trees and flowers and beasts and birds, and every kind of creature, including people. And for many many moons there was peace and harmony in every part of the earth.

~ 2 ~

THE STONE BABY

Cronus now ruled over all that was, and soon he married his sister Rhea, the most beautiful of all the Titans. But he always remembered what he had done to his father Uranus, and he was frightened that one of his own children might do the same to him. So as each child was born, he opened his enormous mouth wide wide wide and swallowed it in one big gulp.

Rhea was very sad that she could never see her children, and she tried to persuade Cronus to let her keep just one. But Cronus just shook his head and patted his big belly.

'They are quite safe in here, my dear,' he boomed. 'I can feel them all wriggling around!'

Rhea decided to ask Gaia for advice.

'When the next child is born, you must play a trick on Cronus,' said Gaia. 'You must get an enormous stone, and wrap it up just like a baby. Keep it beside you, and when Cronus asks you for the child, give him the stone instead, and hide the real baby somewhere safe.' So that is just what Rhea did.

She took the child (whom she named Zeus) to a cave on Mount Ida. Then she summoned some noisy sprites, and told them to play loud music around the cave mouth, so that Cronus wouldn't hear Zeus when he cried. Cronus never noticed a thing. The baby gods and goddesses inside him grew and grew, and kicked and kicked to get out. They used the heavy stone which Rhea had made him swallow as a football inside his tummy, and this made Cronus very cross and uncomfortable as he strode about his business across the heavens and around the earth. And the rumbles his stomach made because of it were the first thunder ever heard.

～ 3 ～

KING OF THE GODS,
LORD OF THE UNIVERSE

Rhea sent a magical goat called Amaltheia and some of her favourite nymphs to look after baby Zeus in the cave on Mount Ida. Amaltheia's milk, which tasted of ambrosia and nectar, made him strong and tall in no time at all, and soon he was as powerful as his great father, Cronus. When Amaltheia died, he gave her horns to the nymphs, to thank them for looking after him so well. They were magic horns of plenty, and whatever food or drink you wished for would pour out of them as soon as you asked for it. Zeus made Amaltheia's skin into magic armour, which nothing could pierce, and strode out into the world.

Rhea sent him a wife, called Metis, who was very wise. Metis told Zeus that he mustn't attack his father until he had some powerful friends to help him, and she knew just how to get them for him by a clever trick.

Zeus hid behind a tree, while Metis dressed up as an

old herbwoman, and waited by the side of the road till Cronus went past.

'Try my herbs of power,' she croaked. 'Never be defeated! Overcome all your enemies!' Cronus was very interested, for lately he had suspected that Rhea was plotting against him.

'I'll take some,' he said, and soon he had swallowed down a big bottle of disgusting green liquid. It was extremely bitter and tasted horrid. All of a sudden he began to feel sick. Then he *was* very sick indeed. Zeus and Metis watched as first a great stone, and then all five of Cronus's other children came up one by one out of his wide wide wide wide mouth. Zeus ran out from behind his tree to join Hades and Poseidon, Hestia, Demeter and Hera, who were all furious with Cronus for trapping them for so long. Cronus took one look at their angry faces and ran away, leaving his powers behind him on the road. Zeus picked them up and put them in his pocket.

'Now *I'm* Lord of the Universe,' he boomed. And all the world heard him, and shivered at his powerful voice.

THE THREE GIFTS

Now that Zeus had picked up his father Cronus's powers, he was the king of heaven and earth and everywhere in between. But even Zeus was not strong enough to look after the universe all by himself. He called his brothers to a meeting.

'I can't rule the universe properly unless you help me,' he said, taking off his helmet. 'Why don't we share it out between us?' Hades and Poseidon agreed, and so into the helmet Zeus put a sapphire for the earth and sky, a

turquoise for the sea, and a ruby for the Underworld. Since Zeus was the most powerful, he closed his eyes and picked first. Out came the sapphire. Poseidon picked the turquoise and Hades the ruby. That was how the division of the universe was decided.

But the Titans, who were Zeus's uncles and aunts, did not like this at all. They thought that *they* should have a share in ruling things, so they raised an army to fight Zeus and his brothers.

Zeus immediately freed the Cyclopes and the hundred-armed monsters that his grandfather had imprisoned in Tartarus, to help him. The Cyclopes were so grateful that they made presents for the brothers.

For Poseidon they made a trident which could cause earthquakes and tidal waves.

For Hades they made a helmet of darkness, so that he could sneak up on his enemies without being seen.

And for Zeus they made thunder and lightning bolts which made him so powerful that no one could stand against him.

The Titans were soon beaten, and Zeus banished nearly all of them to Tartarus, where he set the hundred-armed monsters to guard them. Prometheus and Epimetheus, the only two Titans who had supported

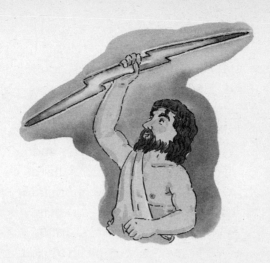

Zeus, were allowed to go free. But Atlas, the strongest of the Titans, was sent to the far ends of the earth, so that he could carry the weight of the heavens on his shoulders forever.

~ 5 ~

THE VOLCANO MONSTER

When Gaia learnt that Zeus had trapped her Titan children in Tartarus, she shook with rage. And out of her raging body there appeared two great and horrible monsters called Typhon and Echidna.

Echidna had a woman's head and arms, but her body was like an enormous fat snake, covered in warty spots and spines.

Typhon had a hundred heads, each one dripping with venom and slime. When he roared like a hundred lions or trumpeted like a herd of elephants, great rivers of boiling mud and fiery stones poured out of his mouths.

When the gods saw him, they were so frightened that they turned themselves into animals and ran far away to hide in the woods.

Typhon tore up enormous mountains by the roots and he hurled them at Zeus and his brothers and sisters, hissing like a thousand snakes. But Zeus was brave, and he called to the other gods to come and help him defeat the monster.

Soon a fierce battle raged over the earth, and everything was destroyed. The gods were tired out and nearly beaten. But as Typhon lifted Mount Etna to throw at Zeus's head, Zeus let fly one of his thunderbolts, and knocked the mountain down on Typhon's heads, trapping him forever.

Echidna fled to a cave in southern Greece when she saw how Zeus had destroyed her mate. There she had her many children, all as hideous as herself, and Zeus allowed them to live in peace, so that the future heroes of Greece could fight them when the time was right.

As for Typhon, he lies wriggling and struggling under Mount Etna to this day, spewing smoke and flames out of the top, and raining down boiling stones on the poor people of Sicily.

~ 6 ~

THE BOY WHO FELL
OUT OF THE SKY

King Minos of Crete was furious. He was seething. He was bubbling with rage. 'Bring me Daedalus!' he cried. Daedalus was the king's inventor, and he had designed an impossible maze to keep the king's Minotaur – a horrible bull monster – safe. Now the monster was dead, the king's only daughter had fled, and Minos wanted someone to blame.

So Daedalus was dragged before King Minos' feet in chains, and after the king had kicked him and jumped on him, he was taken to the highest room in the high-est tower in the palace at Knossos, and locked in with his son, Icarus, who was ten. They had no food, and no water, and soon they were desperately hungry and thirsty. But Daedalus was very clever, and soon he had a plan of escape.

He made Icarus climb up

into the roof, where there was a big old deserted bees' nest. Icarus took all the honeycombs and threw them down to his father. Then he stole the tailfeathers from all the pigeons who were sleeping in the rafters, and threw them down too.

When they had licked some dew off the windowsills and sucked out some honey from the combs, Daedalus melted the beeswax by shining a ray of sun through a magnifying-glass he had in his pocket, and made four big wing shapes out of it. Then, while it was still soft, he pressed the pigeons' feathers into it. He made leather straps from his belt and sandals, and then they were ready.

Daedalus and Icarus strapped their wings onto their shoulders, climbed onto the windowsill, and leapt out into the air. It was quite dark, apart from a few blazing stars, so no one could see them from the ground.

'Wheeee!' shouted Icarus, as he swept through the sky. 'I can fly! Look, Dad! I can fly!'

'Keep going west,' yelled Daedalus, flapping alongside. 'And remember not to fly too high. If the sun catches you when he gets up, he will melt your wings, and you'll fall!'

Icarus was having such a good time he didn't listen. He swooped up to the stars, and pulled Sirius's tail. Then he swooshed round the Great Bear. He didn't notice Helios the sun god driving his great chariot up over the eastern horizon behind him. Helios cracked his whip, and fiery rays of sunshine darted across the sky. One of them touched Icarus's wings, and the beeswax ran like rain down into the ocean far below. A feather brushed Icarus's cheek as he tumbled helplessly to the sea beneath, crying out for his father to save him.

Poor Daedalus could only watch and weep for his lost son as he flew on towards Sicily. As his tears fell into the ocean, they were caught by the nereids and made into pearls of wisdom. And the grandmothers, who know, say that Icarus's spirit rises up from the sea every night, and flies up to the heavens to play with the stars.

~ 7 ~

HOW FIRE CAME
TO EARTH

Zeus wanted to reward Prometheus and Epimetheus, the two Titans who had helped him in battle. So he gave them the job of making new creatures to scamper over the earth, and fill her woods and meadows with songs and joyful sounds once more.

'Here are the things you will need,' he said, pointing to a row of barrels. 'There's plenty for both of you.' And he flew off back to Olympus.

Prometheus set about making some figures out of the first barrel, which was full of clay. He shaped two kinds of bodies, and rolled out long sausages of mud and pressed them against the bodies to make arms and legs. Then he made two round balls, and stuck them on the tops. He hummed as he worked, and his clever fingers shaped ears and eyes and

hair and mouths until the figures looked just like tiny copies of Zeus and his wife. It took him a very long time, because he wanted his creations to be perfect.

In the time that Prometheus had made his two sorts of figures, Epimetheus had made many. First he used up the barrels of spots, then he used all the stripes; he simply flung handfuls of bright feathers about, and as for the whiskers and claws he gave them out twenty at a time! By the time Prometheus had finished his men and women there was not a thing left to give them other than some thin skin, and a little fine hair.

Prometheus went straight to Zeus.

'My creatures are cold!' he said. 'You must give me

some of your special fire to warm them up, or they will die!' But Zeus refused.

'Fire is only for gods. They will just have to manage,' he said. 'You shouldn't have been so slow in making them.'

Now this annoyed Prometheus a lot. He had taken such care, and his creations had things inside that Epimetheus could never even have *thought* of. So he decided to steal Zeus's fire for them. He sneaked up to Olympus, carrying a hollow reed, and stole a glowing coal from Zeus's hearth. Then he flew down to earth.

'Keep this sacred fire of the gods burning always,' he commanded his creatures. And they did. They looked deep into the flames and saw just what they should do. They built temples, and in each temple was a fire. And on the fires they placed offerings to the gods, and the smoke of them reached right up to Zeus's palace on Olympus.

Zeus liked the delicious smell. But when he looked down to earth and saw the fires burning everywhere like little red stars, he was not happy at all.

'Prometheus!' he bellowed. 'I told you not to take that fire! I'll make you regret your stealing ways!' He swooped down on the back of a giant eagle and carried Prometheus away to the Caucasus Mountains, where he chained him to the highest peak. And Zeus sent the giant eagle to visit him every morning and tear enormous chunks out of his liver. Every night the liver magically regrew, so that poor Prometheus's punishment was never-ending.

But Zeus never took back the gift of fire from the earth, and we have it still to warm us on cold winter nights.

~ 8 ~

THE INQUISITIVE WIFE

Pandora was the most inquisitive woman on earth. Zeus had made her that way on purpose. She was always asking questions and prying into other people's business.

'Who's this? What's that? Why? Why? Why?' she would

ask her poor husband Epimetheus at least a hundred times a day. Epimetheus was very patient, and because Pandora was so pretty and he loved her, he put up with her questions. But one day, as she was poking about, Pandora found a great big jar right in the furthest corner of the attic. It was very heavy, and when she tried to lift it, she couldn't. She ran down to Epimetheus, who was talking to some of the animals he had made.

'Husband! Husband!' she squealed as she saw him. 'I've found a lovely big jar, and I want to know what's in it! Come and help me!'

Epimetheus went white as a sheet and began to shake.

'Wife! Wife! You must never never touch that jar! My

brother Prometheus gave it to me, and he made me promise that it must never be moved or opened till the end of the world! Promise me that whatever else you do, you will never touch that jar again!' So Pandora promised, and although it was very difficult for her, she kept her promise for at least an hour. But then, oh dear, her curiosity began to get the better of her.

'Surely if I just have a little tiny peek, it won't do any harm!' she said. And she sneaked up to the attic again.

Pandora quickly took the lid off the jar, and poked her

nose right in. What a horrible surprise she got when a whole lot of nasty looking insects flew out and started pricking her with their stings. She slammed the lid back on at once, shutting inside the only creature that was left.

'Oh! Oh! Oh!' she shrieked as she ran down the stairs past Epimetheus and out into the garden. 'Come and get back in the jar, you horrid little things!' But the insects just buzzed and hummed with shrill little voices and flew off.

Ever since the day Pandora opened that jar, envy and greed, and jealousy and anger and all the other evil things that were shut in there by clever Prometheus have flown about the world, stinging human beings and pricking them all over with their sharp little pins. Only hope was left in the jar – trapped by Pandora right at the very bottom. And as long as hope is there, nothing in the world can ever be quite as bad as it seems.

THE GREATEST FLOOD

Prometheus had a son called Deucalion, who was good and kind. He loved all the birds and beasts and insects – he even loved the eagle who tore at his father's liver each morning.

'He's only doing his job!' he would say to poor

Prometheus, on his yearly visit to the Caucasus. And Prometheus would grit his teeth and nod bravely, as Deucalion stroked the eagle's feathers while they talked.

But one year, Prometheus was brought some terrible tidings by the North Wind. He begged the eagle to take a day off to fetch Deucalion to him. And because Deucalion had been kind to him, the eagle went.

'My son,' said Prometheus. 'You must save yourself and your wife. Zeus is angry with Pandora for opening my jar and letting all the evils into the world. They have infected my clay people, and now they are being so cruel to each other that Zeus is going to get rid of them. He is going to make it rain and rain, till all the earth

is covered, and everything in it is drowned. You must make a boat for yourself and Pyrrha and then you will escape.'

'But Father, what about all the animals and birds and insects? They aren't like your people – they are innocent. How can I save *them*?' asked Deucalion.

So Prometheus told him how to build a great ark, with enough room for two of each kind of creature. And soon the whole earth was covered in water, and the only things alive upon it were Deucalion and his wife, and the creatures they had gathered into the ark. It was very smelly, and there wasn't much food, but after nine nights and days the waters went down, and the ark came to land on the top of a great mountain.

The animals and birds and insects scampered and flew and crawled off to find new homes, and Deucalion and Pyrrha knelt on the land and praised Zeus for their escape. They lit a fire with some precious embers they had saved in a pot, and as the smoke reached up to Olympus, Zeus looked down and saw them praying.

'These are good people,' he thought. 'I shall help them.' So he gave a message to the North Wind, Boreas, and sent him to blow it into Deucalion's ear.

'Zeus says to throw the mother's bones over your shoulder!' whistled Boreas. Deucalion was very surprised. Surely Zeus didn't mean Pyrrha's bones.

'Zeus means the bones of Mother Earth, silly!' said Pyrrha. And she picked up a big stone and threw it over her shoulder. Immediately, a little girl stood there. She came running up to Pyrrha to be hugged.

Deucalion and Pyrrha walked all over the earth throwing stones over their shoulders, and in each place they walked Deucalion made men and Pyrrha made women. Some were brown and some were pink, and some were yellow and some were black. And because they were made from stone, Pandora's evil stinging insects were not nearly so harmful to them as they had been to the people Prometheus had made of clay so many years before.

THE CUCKOO'S TRICK

Zeus was brave, he was strong, he was handsome – in fact he was the greatest of the gods. So why wouldn't beautiful Hera marry him? He brought her magical flowers that bloomed a different colour each day. He brought her crowns made of moonbeams and necklaces made of starlight. But Hera just looked down her long

straight perfect nose and laughed.

'Oh Zeus!' she sighed. 'Just leave me alone and go and play with your thunderbolts. I'll never marry you until you can sit on my lap without me noticing – and that will be never!' And Zeus stomped back to his palace in a terrible temper that made the earth below shake and tremble.

Then he had an idea. He would do just what Hera had told him. He *would* go and play with his thunderbolts. Zeus stirred up the most tremendous thunderstorm that ever was. Then he changed himself into a cuckoo, and set out for Hera's palace through the storm. Wet, bedraggled and exhausted, he flew through the window of her bedroom, and landed shaking on her bed.

'Poor little cuckoo!' said Hera, stroking his soaking grey feathers. 'Let me dry you.' In no time at all the cuckoo was dry and comfortable, and nestling into Hera's lap. Then the cuckoo began to change. It grew and grew until – there was Zeus sitting in Hera's lap, laughing.

'Cuckoo!' he said, kissing her. 'Will you marry me now?' And Hera had to agree.

Zeus and Hera were given many amazing wedding presents by all the gods and goddesses, in celebration of their marriage. The most wonderful of all was the magical apple tree given to Hera by Mother Earth. Its fruit was as golden as the sun, and it gave everlasting life to anyone who ate it. Hera planted it in her special garden, and set three beautiful nymphs to guard it, together with Argos, the hundred-eyed monster who never slept. In later times Heracles, the bravest hero of all, stole some of the precious apples, but that is quite another story.

THE QUEEN OF THE UNDERWORLD

Demeter, goddess of the harvest, had hair the colour of sunset, and lips and cheeks as pink and perfect as a summer morning. Wherever she walked on the earth, trees would burst into fruit, and corn ripen to burning gold; flowers would waft sweet scents towards her, and vegetables swell and pop with green juicy life.

She had a daughter called Kore, the most lovely child ever born, and it was Demeter's delight to play with her all the long sunny days of summer – and where Demeter was it was always summer. But when Kore was about sixteen years old, she was seen picking flowers in the fields and woods by Hades, the dark god of the Underworld. Hades fell in love with her at once, but he knew that Demeter would never give permission for him to marry her – he would have to kidnap her instead.

So one bright afternoon Hades drove his chariot pulled by six black horses out of a huge crack in the ground, seized Kore in his arms, and carried her off screaming to his kingdom of Tartarus, deep in the Underworld. Only a little shepherd boy and his brother had seen what had happened and they were too scared to say anything.

For a whole year Demeter travelled in search of her daughter, calling and calling. And while she called, tears ran down her face so fast that it became all wrinkled and crinkled, and her lovely hair turned grey and lank with sadness. Nothing grew or bloomed any more, and the earth became a frozen, dark place, where the North Wind blew snow and ice over the fields, and no birds sang. Men, women and children shivered and shook as they huddled round their fires and starved.

In the heavens, only Helios the sun god had seen what Hades had done. He told Zeus, but as usual, Zeus decided not to interfere with his dark brother's doings. However he soon noticed how cold and unhappy the mortals on earth were. There were no nice-smelling sacrifices to the gods, no prayers, only misery. He saw at once that he would have to do something after all, and so he sent his messenger, Hermes, to comfort Demeter.

'Don't you worry, my dear. I'll get her back for you,' said Hermes, who had just talked to the two shepherd boys and found out where Kore was. And down he went to visit Hades, down down down to Tartarus in the deepest part of the earth, where the dead souls of men and heroes wander like mist.

Now it is well known that if you eat any food from the Underworld, you can never return to the earth. Kore knew this, and so although Hades had tempted her with delicious food and drink, she had not touched a single morsel in all the time she had been there. All she had eaten was three seeds from a pomegranate growing in Hades' garden, when she thought nobody was looking.

When Hermes came to demand that Kore be returned to her mother, Hades smiled a nasty smile.

'Little Kore has been very silly!' he smirked. 'She thought nobody would see her. But my gardener was hiding behind a tree, and he swears he saw her spit three pomegranate pips into a bush!' Kore burst into tears. Now she would never escape from her dreary prison, where the sun never shone, and the only birdsong was the cawing of ravens.

But Hermes was very crafty.

'If you don't send Kore back to Demeter, everyone on earth will die from cold and starvation, and you will be so busy sorting the dead souls out that you won't have time to even think, let alone enjoy yourself. Why don't you let her spend a month here for every seed she ate, and the rest with her mother up on the earth?'

Hades knew when he was beaten, and he agreed to Hermes' plan. So Kore went back to her mother for nine months of the year, and the earth bloomed once more. But for the three months that we call winter, Kore now changes her name to Persephone, and goes to live with Hades underground. And the cold winds blow, and the snow falls, and Demeter weeps tears of ice because she misses her daughter so much.

~ 12 ~

THE FOAM GODDESS

Many years ago, when Uranus fled into the deepest heavens, one drop of blood from the great wound that his son, Cronus, had given him dripped into the sea and changed into foam.

'We must not waste this precious gift,' whispered the waves. And they rushed at the magic foam, and swirled it and whirled it into the shape of the most beautiful goddess of all, Aphrodite. A giant scallop shell was brought up from the depths of the ocean on the back of a whale, and six dolphins were harnessed to it. Then Aphrodite stepped into it and settled onto its pink velvety cushions while she was blown to the shores of the island of Cythera by the West Wind. As she stepped onto the earth for the first time, clouds of sparrows and doves flew twittering and cooing round her head, and three lovely maidens brought her robes made of sea-spray and rainbows.

When Zeus saw her exquisite beauty, he knew that all the gods would fight over her, so he quickly married her off to his son, the lame blacksmith god Hephaestus.

'That will keep her out of trouble,' he thought to

himself. Aphrodite was not at all happy about this, for Hephaestus was always black and sooty from the dirt of his forge fires.

'Ugh! Get off!' she snarled, as he kissed her on their

wedding night. 'Look at your dirty fingerprints all over my clean robe!'

She would much rather have married his brother, handsome Ares, or funny Hermes who teased her and made her laugh. But Aphrodite soon came round when she saw the beautiful things that Hephaestus made for her. The most wonderful of all was a magic golden girdle, set with glittering jewels. Whenever Aphrodite wore it, she was so lovely that no one could resist anything she asked, not even if it was Zeus himself.

Although she lived on Olympus, Aphrodite always went back to her birthplace for a month's holiday every year. And when she came back to her palace, the very flowers bowed beneath her feet in amazement at her shining beauty and grace. She had a little son called Eros whom she thought was the most beautiful child in the world. Together they danced across the earth and the heavens shooting gods and mortals alike with their arrows of love, and as they passed, even the cold hearts of the stars were filled with joy.

~ 13 ~

THE LAME BLACKSMITH

Hephaestus was the son of Zeus and Hera. As a baby, he was rather small and puny, and he didn't like loud noises. So when his father threw thunderbolts, and his mother shouted, he cowered in his cradle and shivered.

As a little boy, though, he grew braver, and one day when his parents were arguing, he tried to stop them.

'You hurt my ears!' he said, glaring at Zeus. 'Why don't you both just stop shouting – Yack! Bang! Yell! Yack! Bang! Yell! – I'm fed up with listening to you.' Now this made Zeus so angry that he picked Hephaestus up by his ears and flung him down to earth.

Hephaestus fell for a whole day, and when he landed feet first on the island of Lemnos, his leg bones shattered into tiny pieces, and he fainted from the pain. There Thetis the sea-nymph found him, and carried him to

her cave, where she and her daughter looked after him for nine whole years. Because Hephaestus was now lame, and couldn't get around easily, he amused himself by making beautiful things with his strong hands, and soon he was the cleverest smith and jeweller that ever lived.

One day Hera met Thetis at a party, and admired her dolphin brooch, made of sea pearls and sapphires.

'Where did you get that?' she asked. 'I must have one myself!' When she discovered that it was her own son who was the craftsman, she carried him straight to Olympus and made Zeus apologise and set him up as official blacksmith to the gods. Zeus was very sorry for what he had done, and that was why he chose Hephaestus to be Aphrodite's husband.

Hephaestus built a smithy deep in the heart of the mountains, with twenty bellows worked by the Cyclopes, who became his assistants. Among the amazing things he made were two robots of silver and gold, which would do anything he asked. And when the gods had meetings, they used his little magic tables, which ran around on golden wheels, taking food and drink to anyone who needed it.

～ 14 ～

THE BULL FROM
THE SEA

Zeus loved his birthplace, Crete. He knew every rocky inch of it, the way the hills smelled of thyme in the sunshine, the way the dark sea sounded when it rushed against the shore. He knew the little white villages, and the narrow ledges where the seagulls nested, and the caves where bats hung from dark crevices in the stone.

'Crete needs a queen,' he thought one day, as he flew back to Olympus. 'But where can I find a woman good and beautiful enough to take care of my beloved island for me?' Zeus looked and looked whenever he visited earth. But every woman he saw was either too tall or too short, too fat or too thin, too chatty or too silent. Not one woman came close to what he wanted until one day, flying over the city of Tyre, he saw a girl playing on the seashore with some of her friends.

'Ha!' said Zeus, making himself invisible. 'This is the one. She's perfect!'

Europa was the King of Tyre's daughter. She had long dark hair as shiny as chestnuts, and grey eyes that turned as blue as dye when she was happy. They were blue now, but they quickly changed back to grey as she looked at the sea and saw a great white bull wading up towards her out of the waves. At first, Europa and her friends were frightened, but when the bull lay down quietly on the shore and looked at them through his long silky eyelashes, they came closer and stroked his furry flanks. The bull snorted softly, and his breath smelled of violets.

'Ooh, isn't he sweet?' squealed Europa. 'Do let's make some garlands for his horns, and then we can take him back to the palace and keep him as a pet!' So the girls ran into the meadows by the beach and picked some sea pinks and cistus and wove them into garlands. Europa was the tallest, so she climbed onto the bull's broad back to slip them over his sharp horns. As she knelt astride his shoulders, the bull got up and started to gallop out to sea along a great road of shining water that had suddenly appeared. Europa's friends screamed and ran after him

into the waves, but it was no good – the bull had vanished as quickly as he had come.

Europa was a brave girl, so she was not a bit surprised when the bull spoke to her as he ran.

'I am Zeus, greatest of the gods,' he bellowed. 'I have chosen you to be Queen of Crete. I shall marry you as my mortal wife, and we will have fine sons together.'

And what Zeus said came true. After he had married Europa, and given her a crown of beautiful jewels, they had three strong sons. Europa ruled happily in the palace Zeus built for her, and she was helped by a marvellous bronze robot called Talos, which Hephaestus had made for her on Zeus's orders. Talos clanked around the island on his metal legs three times a day, and if an enemy ship came near, he threw rocks at it. Together, Talos and Europa kept Crete safe from any enemies for many long years.

THE COPPER TOWER

King Acrisius of Argos was the most super-stitious man in the world. He saw omens in the moon and stars; if his ships needed wind for their sails he whistled for it, and if he walked under a ladder, he stayed in bed for a week to avoid bad luck.

Now Acrisius had a daughter called Danäe, who was the apple of his eye. 'Hello, my flower!' he would say every morning. 'Come and give your old father a kiss.' But when Danäe was about seventeen, a soothsayer came to Argos, and demanded to tell the king's fortune. He was rather grubby, with a hat hung with rats' tails and a necklace of wild animal teeth. The king was just about to offer him a goblet of wine, and ask what he could do for him, when the soothsayer swayed in front of him and started to dribble and foam at the mouth.

'Beware, oh King, beware!' he wailed. 'For your flower will give birth to a seed, and when the seed is grown, then you will die!' And with that, he turned and ran from the room as fast as a leopard.

Acrisius was horrified, but it was quite obvious what the man had meant. So he shut Danaë up in a tower which he covered from top to bottom in copper, so that no one could get in or out. Only a small flap at the foot for food and a small hole in the roof for air were left, and no one could have got through those.

'Now she will never have children,' said the king. 'And I shall live forever!' But Zeus was passing by as Acrisius spoke, and the king's words made him very angry.

'We shall see about that,' he roared in Acrisius's frightened ear. 'For only the gods can make you immortal, and I don't think *you* deserve it!' And with that he changed himself into a shower of golden rain and dived through the hole in the roof of Danaë's tower.

Danaë was very pleased to see the pretty raindrops, and they danced and played with her all day long. In due course, Danaë gave birth to a baby boy called Perseus, but Danaë always thought of him as her little rainbow.

Acrisius didn't dare to offend Zeus by harming his grandchild, because he knew that Perseus was Zeus's son. But he knew he had to get rid of him. So at dead of night he and his soldiers made a big hole in the tower, and dragged Perseus and Danaë out. They were bundled into a large chest, and thrown off the harbour wall into the sea below.

'That way,' thought Acrisius, 'if anything bad happens I can blame it on Poseidon.' And he went back to his palace and climbed into bed.

The chest tossed and tumbled through the waves at first. But Zeus sent some nymphs to carry it through the sea, and soon the chest bumped up against the shores of Seriphos. A very wet Danäe, clutching a cold and crying baby, climbed out onto the shore of the island. Just then, a poor shepherd passed by, and saw her standing there shivering. He took off his cloak and wrapped her and Perseus in it. Then he took them back to his cottage, and they lived there happily for many years until Perseus grew up into a handsome young man and went off on his adventures.

～ 16 ～

THE SNAKE-HAIRED GORGON

The king of Seriphos wanted to marry Princess Danäe, but she didn't want to marry him at all. So Perseus, Danäe's son by Zeus, went to the king and asked him to find someone else to marry. The king pretended to agree, but what he really wanted was to get Perseus out of the way.

'I suppose I *could* marry another princess,' he said. 'But you will have to go off and do some very difficult task to make up for my disappointment.' Perseus would have done anything to save his mother, and he said so.

'Very well,' said the king nastily. 'You shall go and kill the Gorgon Medusa for me.'

'Never mind, mother!' said Perseus as he told Danäe the news. 'Surely this old Gorgon can't be too hard to kill. I'll just sneak up on her somehow, and chop her head off while she isn't looking.' But Danäe just wailed harder. In fact she wailed so hard that Zeus himself heard her, and looked down from Olympus.

Now Zeus didn't like the king of Seriphos, and because Perseus was his own son, he decided to give him some help. As Perseus set out on his journey, leaving his weeping mother behind, two shining figures appeared on the road in front of him.

'Hail, Perseus!' said the first, a beautiful woman with an owl on her shoulder. 'I am Athene.' And she gave him a magic shield, all polished like a mirror.

'Hail, Perseus!' said the second, a cheeky-looking youth with a winged hat on his curly head, and winged sandals on his feet. 'I am Hermes.' And he handed Perseus a magical sword with the words *'Hard as a diamond though it be, the hardest thing can be cut by me!'* engraved on its blade.

'These will help you against the Gorgon Medusa,' said Hermes. 'But you need three more magical things if you are to succeed, and they are held by the Nymphs of the North. The only people who know where their house is are the Three Grey Women, who are Medusa's sisters. If you come with me, and do just as I say, I can trick them into telling you the way.'

Perseus was so amazed by his good luck that he just stood there with his mouth open.

Hermes took his hand, and away they flew together, up up up into the blue sky, on on on till the earth changed to white beneath them and the clouds turned dark and sulky above.

The Three Grey Women were quarrelling when Perseus and Hermes landed behind their hut at dusk.

'It's my turn!' shrieked the eldest, who was thin and wispy with long tangled hair and fingernails like rusty swords.

'No! Mine!' screeched the middle sister, who was dumpy and bedraggled, with ears like slimy grey slugs.

'You can't have them till tomorrow!' hissed the youngest, who was completely bald, with a nose like a vulture's beak.

'They only have one eye and one tooth between them,' whispered Hermes, 'and they're always fighting over them. Now, while I distract the Grey Women, you go and snatch them, and then we can bargain.' He stepped out from behind the hut.

'Good morning!' said Hermes, grinning. And he produced a long feather from behind his back and began to tickle the sisters all over. They laughed so much that the eye and tooth fell out of the youngest one's grasp, and rolled towards Perseus, who picked them up and put them in his pocket.

'Time for business!' said Hermes. 'Where are the Nymphs of the North!'

'WE'LL NEVER TELL YOU!' yelled the sisters. Hermes sighed.

'Then we'll just have to drop your eye and tooth in the sea,' he said. There was dead silence and then all three sisters began babbling.

'Left at the ash tree . . . straight on till Dragon Mountain . . . past the Sea of Serpents and it's first on the right.'

'Thank you!' said Hermes, soaring into the air with Perseus. 'Now catch!' And he took the eye and tooth from Perseus and threw them to the ground. The shrieks and curses followed them for miles.

The Nymphs of the North welcomed Perseus, and gladly gave him the magical leather bag, winged sandals and cap of invisibility which he needed.

'Where are you?' asked Hermes, after he had put them on.

'Up here!' laughed the invisible Perseus from above the treetops. And off he flew to look for Medusa, with Hermes's last words floating up to him.

'Use your shield as a mirror to look at the Gorgons, or you will be turned to stone! And remember, Medusa is the only one that looks human!'

After flying for a very long way, he saw a rocky little island thousands of feet below. There was a beach of snowy white sand on the far side, and fast asleep by a cave in the cliffs lay three monsters. They were covered in gigantic greeny-bronze insect scales, and their long thin golden wings rose and fell as they breathed. Instead of hair they all had snakes growing from their heads, writing and hissing as they slept.

Perseus looked at them carefully in his shield mirror. Which was Medusa? As the monsters sighed and turned over, he saw that the nearest had the face of a beautiful woman. Perseus landed softly and raised his sword, taking careful aim in the mirror. The sword snickered through the silent air and cut down to the sand beneath, as Medusa's head rolled off her shoulders and landed with a thump at his feet. Quickly he opened the magic bag, which stretched itself to the right size at once, and stuffed Medusa's head inside. He felt the snakes wriggling as he attached it to his belt and flew towards the sun.

At that moment the other Gorgons woke up and found their sister dead. How their talons clawed and scratched the air as they flapped round the island, shrieking horribly and looking for someone to turn to stone. But the invisible Perseus fled hurriedly in the other direction, the Gorgon's head safe at his side.

~ 17 ~

THE MAGIC HEAD

The wind blew and the lightning flashed, and Perseus was blown this way and that, through thunder and clouds and rain, till he didn't know which way was up. He clutched his precious bag with one hand and his cap of invisibility with the other, and prayed to Zeus to save him. But Zeus had sent the storm on purpose.

As soon as Perseus was over the coast of Ethiopia, the wind died, and the sun came out in a sky as blue as delphiniums. Looking down, he saw a great rock. Something was moving on the top of it, and Perseus flew down to have a closer look. There, chained to a post, was the loveliest girl he had ever seen.

'Who are you, and what are you doing here?' he asked as he landed, and took off his cap. The girl screamed as he appeared, but when he had calmed her down, she told him that she was Andromeda, the daughter of the king and queen, and that she had been left as a sacrifice to Poseidon, the god of the sea, whom her mother had offended.

'Run for your life,' she said. 'A monster is coming to eat me up, and if you stay here you will be killed as well!' But Perseus had fallen in love with Andromeda, and was

determined to save her if he could. So he hid behind a
rock and waited.

Soon a great roiling and boiling in the sea started, and
a huge warty head appeared, with trails of seaweed and
slime hanging from it. The monster opened its mouth,
and showed its teeth, each one as long as a man's arm. As
Andromeda cowered away, Perseus ran forward with his
magic sword and plunged it into the creature's throat. It
nearly bit his arm off as it reared away, roaring and
pouring blood into the water.

With the monster dead, Perseus cut through
Andromeda's chains, and they flew to her father's palace.
The king and queen were surprised and delighted to see

their daughter alive, and agreed that Perseus could marry her at once. But just then in came the man who had been engaged to Andromeda before she had gone off to be sacrificed. He was furious at the king and queen's decision, and rushed at Perseus with his sword raised. Perseus whipped Medusa's head out of his bag, and in a trice the man was turned to stone.

Andromeda and Perseus returned to Seriphos, but Danäe was nowhere to be found. The king of Seriphos had tried to marry her again, and she had gone into hiding.

'How dare he annoy my mother!' roared Perseus. And he marched into the throne room and thrust Medusa's head into the king's surprised face, turning him to stone at once.

The people of Seriphos were happy, because the king had been cruel to all of them. His stone body was thrown into the harbour, and Perseus and Andromeda were crowned king and queen in his place. Danäe came

out of hiding, and the joyful hugging and feasting and laughter went on for weeks and weeks. Perseus soon gave Medusa's head and the other magical things back to the gods. And he was so happy that he vowed never to go on any adventures again.

THE ROBBER'S BED

In the far-off days of his youth, King Aegeus had been secretly married to a beautiful princess of Troezen called Aethra. He had had to leave her behind when he went back to rule Athens, but he never forgot her.

'I shall leave my golden sword and sandals under this great boulder, my darling,' he said as he kissed her goodbye. 'If we should have a son who is strong enough to get them out, then send him to me, and I shall make him my heir.'

In due course, Aethra had a son called Theseus (the one who later killed the Cretan Minotaur). When he was eighteen years old his mother called him to her.

'That boulder in the garden is annoying me,' she said. 'Could you just move it for me?' Theseus always obeyed his mother, so he put his back against the boulder and pushed. It didn't move. He pushed harder. The boulder moved a fraction. He pushed with all his strength. The boulder toppled over and rolled into the valley below with a crash.

Aethra stepped forward, picked

up the golden sword and sandals and gave them to Theseus. 'These belonged to your father, King Aegeus. Take them to him in Athens. He will know where they came from.' So Theseus packed a bag, kissed his mother and set off to Athens.

He had many adventures along the way, but the strangest of all happened near a place called Corydallus, just outside Athens. As Theseus was walking along, he came to a deep wooded valley. It was dark and gloomy, and no birds sang in the trees. The rain dripped from the leaves in heavy drops and soon Theseus was soaked. As night was falling fast, he was very glad to come to a little hut in a clearing with a long bench outside.

'Hey!' he called at the door. 'Is anyone there?' At once a strange old man pranced out. He had a great black beard, and huge arms like treetrunks, but his legs were spindly and thin, and he was completely bald.

'Have you come to try my famous bed, young sir?' he said with a cackle.

Now this old man's name was Procrustes, and he was a very famous robber. He offered lonely travellers supper and the use of his bed for the night. Then he killed them and stole their gold.

Theseus was very tired, so he ate a good supper and then lay down to sleep. His feet dangled over the edge of the bed. Soon he was woken by Procrustes singing softly to himself.

> *Chop the tall ones, make them fit,*
> *Cut them up, then wait a bit.*

Poke them to make sure they're dead,
Steal their gold, then make the bed!
Stretch the short ones till they're tall,
Tie them up then give a haul,
Wait till bones go crick and crack,
Put their gold in a great big sack!

Theseus didn't like Procrustes' song one little bit. He had heard the stories about people disappearing around here, and now he knew why. He leaped out of bed and grabbed the old man.

'You will never kill another innocent traveller,' he cried. And *snicker-snacker-snick* he chopped Procrustes

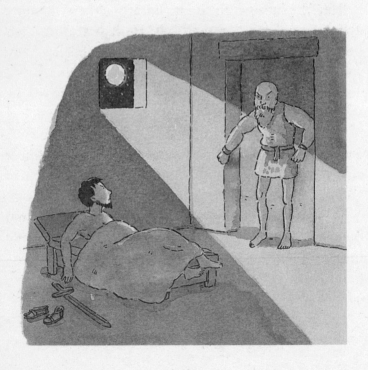

into tiny little bits with the golden sword before he could sing another note.

When Theseus arrived at Athens, poor King Aegeus wept as he saw his old sword and sandals. 'My son,' he cried. 'You are just in time to sail to Crete and save us from the dreadful Minotaur!' So brave Theseus went straight off to Crete without ever getting to know his father properly, and of course by the time he returned, King Aegeus was dead. But that is another story for another time and another place, because now it's time for bed.

~ 19 ~

THE MONSTER IN
THE MAZE

The breeze brought the news. First it was a whisper in the trees, then it crept through the gates and blew against the palace windows.

'Theseus has returned!' it said. At first the people did not believe it, for what good luck could come to a city that had been cursed for eighteen long years? But then the palace trumpets blew, and the heralds went through the streets, and the people finally believed that King Aegeus's lost son had come back to them at last.

'Maybe he will stop the monster eating our children,' they muttered to one another. 'Maybe he is the hero we have been waiting for.'

In the royal palace of Athens Theseus looked at the father he had only just found. 'You want me to sail to Crete and kill the Minotaur?' he asked. 'But why?' King Aegeus pulled at his long beard despairingly.

'For eighteen years King Minos has demanded a terrible sacrifice from us. Every nine years we have to send seven girls and seven boys to be eaten up by his dreadful monster, the Minotaur, otherwise he will send his armies to kill us all. You are strong and clever. If you go with them, you may be able to think of some way of saving us.'

Early next morning, a fleet of black-sailed ships set out for Crete.

'Goodbye, people of Athens!' shouted Theseus from the deck. 'If I succeed, we will hoist white sails for our return. If the sails are still black, you will know I have failed.'

When the ships reached Crete, the harbour walls were packed with faces as the thirteen children and Theseus landed. Each of them wore a garland of flowers as they were led towards King Minos's dungeons. Theseus looked up, and standing on a wall he saw the most lovely girl. Their eyes met, and she smiled at him. Theseus's heart pounded – he was in love at once.

The dungeons were dark and smelly, and that evening Theseus paced up and down as he tried to think of a plan. Suddenly, he heard a whisper.

'Psst!' it said. 'Come to the window!'

'Quick! Help me up!' said Theseus to the boy next to him, and the boy pushed him up to the tiny barred opening, where he clung on tightly. Just outside stood the lovely girl!

'I am Ariadne, the king's daughter, and I've come to save you!' Theseus was amazed.

'But how?' he whispered back.

Ariadne handed him something through the window. 'I made Daedalus give me this. He's my father's inventor. It's magic string. It can never get tangled up. If you tie

one end to your belt, and drop the ball as you go into the maze, you can find your way back by following the thread.' Then she handed him a sharp dagger. 'Kill the Minotaur with this, and when you come back I will be waiting with your friends and we can escape together. I hate my father for his cruelty, and I want to run away with you.'

Soon Theseus heard the clank of armour coming along the passage. He hid the magic string and the dagger in his vest.

'Now then, who's first?' asked a rough-looking soldier. Theseus stepped forward.

'Don't worry!' he said to the children, who were shivering and crying in a corner. The soldier laughed

cruelly as he dragged him through the deserted passages.

'In there!' he said, pushing Theseus through a large iron door and slamming it shut. There was a dreadful bellowing noise coming from somewhere inside, but Theseus quickly tied the string to his belt, dropped the ball, and walked forward. The thread unrolled behind him.

The labyrinth twisted and turned, so that Theseus became confused. The roaring got louder and louder, making the floor and walls shake, and soon he could hear words.

'Meat! Meat! Want man meat to eat!' All at once, a monster burst round the corner. It had the body of a man and the head of a bull, and its jaws were dripping with red foam. Theseus ran towards it with his dagger clenched in his teeth, swung himself up on its huge horns, and leapt onto its back. The Minotaur bellowed again and tried to shake him off, but Theseus took his

dagger and stabbed it till it was dead. Then he followed the string back through the twists and turns of the maze to the great iron door. It was still closed.

'Let me out!' he whispered, knocking on it softly. And like a miracle, it opened. There was Ariadne, standing with the thirteen children behind her. The rough soldier lay snoring on the floor, a cup of drugged wine by his side.

Quickly they ran through the darkness to the waiting ships. The sails were soon up, and they were sailing away, safe at last!

As dawn rose, they landed on the island of Naxos. Theseus was just about to take Ariadne in his arms and kiss her when a shining ball of light appeared before them. Out stepped the god Dionysius, and snatched Ariadne from Theseus.

'You may not marry her!' said the god. 'For Zeus has written her name in the stars, and she is to be my queen!' Theseus knew that gods are not to be argued with, so he bowed his head and walked sadly back to his ships. In fact he was so sad that he forgot to change the sails on the ships from black to white.

Every day King Aegeus stood on the high cliffs of Sounion, watching for his son. When he saw the black sails on the horizon he gave a great wail of despair, and threw himself down into the sea below. Although there was great rejoicing at the Minotaur's defeat, the people wept for their poor dead king. They named the sea in which he had drowned the Aegean in his honour. Theseus became king and ruled Athens well for many long years. But he never saw Ariadne again. She married Dionysius, and in the end he made her very happy. And when she died, Zeus took her crown and hung it among the stars, so that her name should never be forgotten.

20

THE MAN WHO LOVED THE MOON

Endymion the shepherd tapped his fingers. Then he twirled his thumbs. Then he counted the wrinkles on his knuckles. His flute was broken, his knife was blunt, and he was bored bored bored with sitting and looking at sheep sheep sheep the whole day long. His father, Zeus, was the ruler of all the gods, and he was allowed to throw thunderbolts and fight giants. So why was it that the handsomest young man in Caria was only allowed to look after a flock of smelly animals?

At dusk, he set off home, driving the sheep in front of him. Their bells rang sweetly as they walked. Just as he reached the top of the hill, he noticed a beautiful woman standing there. She had the full moon behind her, and she shone with a pearly light that lit up her long hair and her mysterious black eyes. Endymion stared.

'Who are you?' he whispered, falling to his knees. The woman glided over and took his hands. Raising him up, she looked into his face and smiled.

'I am Selene, goddess of the Moon,' she said. 'And I will love you forever.'

Endymion forgot his sheep and his boredom; he forgot everything except Selene. She took him to a cave on Mount Latmus, and there they spent many loving hours together. But Selene was not happy. She loved Endymion so much that she did not want him to grow old and die. So while he slept, she flew up to Zeus.

'Your son is so beautiful,' she said. 'Please enchant him so that he can never change, and I shall have him forever!' So Zeus went with her to the cave, and there he enchanted Endymion and put him into an eternal sleep. Every night Selene kissed him as she entered his dreams and in time they had fifty lovely daughters together, each more beautiful than the last.

THE GOLDEN KING
AND THE ASSES' EARS

Old Silenus the satyr was a bit wobbly. He'd had a party the night before with some nymphs and now his horns hurt and his hooves were tired, and he needed somewhere to sleep. He noticed a nice comfortable looking flowerbed nearby, and settled himself down for a nap.

King Midas was counting his gold when he heard the commotion. Three guards appeared in the throne room, dragging Silenus between them.

'Found him in the garden, your Majesty,' said the captain.

'Asleep in your best violets, your Majesty,' said the corporal.

'All squashed they are now, your Majesty,' said the private.

Now King Midas rather liked satyrs, so instead of punishing Silenus, he put him to bed and sent a message to the god Dionysius to come and collect him. As it happened, Silenus was a favourite of Dionysius's, so he offered King Midas a reward for his kindness.

'Whatever you like,' said the god. 'Just ask.'

King Midas had a passion for gold. He was very rich, but he had never had enough to satisfy him. 'I want everything I touch to turn to gold,' he said.

'Are you *quite* sure?' asked Dionysius. King Midas nodded. 'Very well then,' said the god, waving his hand.

As soon as Dionysius had left, King Midas ran around the room, touching everything. Quite soon the room was a-sparkle and a-gleam with gold.

The curtains, the chairs, the table, the walls – everything was made of gold.

'Hooray!' shouted King Midas. 'I'm rich!' Just then his servants came in to bring him his dinner. But as he grabbed a piece of roast goat to put in his mouth, there was a clang, and a bit of tooth dropped onto the table. The roast goat had turned to gold. Quickly, Midas poured himself some wine. But as he put it to his lips, the liquid turned to solid gold too.

'Oh dear,' said King Midas. 'Now what shall I do?' As he spoke, his little daughter ran in to say goodnight. The minute he had kissed her, he backed away in horror, for she had turned stiff and golden in an instant.

'NO!' he cried. 'Dionysius, please, take this gift away!' Dionysius stepped out from behind a pillar.

'Tell me what is more precious,' he asked. 'A piece of bread or a lump of gold? A drink of water, or a golden

cup? A child's smile, or a golden statue?' Midas fell to his knees.

'I never want to see gold again,' he wept. 'Tell me how I can get rid of it!'

'You must go to the river and bathe in it. Then you must pour river water over everything you have touched,' said the god. Midas ran to the river at once. Oh how glad he was when his daughter smiled and laughed as the water ran off her nightdress. Oh how happy he was to eat soggy goat's meat and drink watery wine. He vowed never to touch gold again, and he didn't.

But he did do one more stupid thing.

Pan the goat god had boasted that his pipes sounded better than Apollo's lyre, and they had agreed that King Midas was to be the judge. Tootle-toot, went Pan. Plinkety-plink, went Apollo. Now Midas didn't want to offend either god, but Apollo was playing a golden lyre. Midas shuddered as he looked at it, because it reminded him of Dionysius's gift.

'Apollo's lyre sounds like a tinkling crystal stream,' he said, 'but Pan's pipes sound like the sweetest bird. I award the prize to Pan.' Of course Apollo was furious.

'The man's an ass!' he shouted crossly. 'And he shall have asses' ears to prove it!' Right there and then large hairy ears sprouted from King Midas's head.

'What shall I do? Whatever shall I do?' he moaned, hiding his head in a curtain. Luckily his queen was very clever, and she designed a special tall cap to cover his ears, so that no one would ever know. The lords and ladies of the court thought the cap was very smart, so they all copied it.

Only King Midas's hairdresser was let into the secret, and he promised never to tell on pain of death. But over the years, the secret became heavier and heavier inside him until it was like a great lump of lead in his stomach.

'I've got to tell!' he groaned. 'I've got to!' So he dug a little hole by the river and whispered the secret into it. But the wind carried the secret to the reeds, and the reeds rustled it to the birds, and soon the whole world knew that King Midas had asses' ears. All his subjects laughed at him, but they all still wear the cap his wife invented to this very day.

22

THE GRASSHOPPER HUSBAND

Eos lived in a palace to the east of the east of the world. The walls were made of mother of pearl, and the doors of rosepetals. The curtains were spun from cloud shadows, and the carpets woven from the softness of sky. Early each morning, Eos got out of her bed and hung her huge fluffy pink pillows out of the window to be blown about by her sons, the winds. Then she drew a bucket of dew from her magic well, and washed herself all over. The sparkling drops flew down to earth, to tell the world that day had come.

One afternoon, Eos woke from a nap in her garden and as she stepped out of her hammock, she looked down to earth and saw a most beautiful young man. His name was Prince Tithonus, and as soon as Eos saw him she knew she must have him for her husband. She put on her best silver slippers and her

best dress, and went to see Zeus.

'Well,' said Zeus gruffly. 'Marry him if you must, but don't come running to me for any more favours. Hera's not in a very good mood just now, and she wouldn't like it. I shall give him eternal life for a wedding present, and that will have to do.'

So Eos married Tithonus, and they lived happily in Eos's palace without a care in the world. But although Zeus had given Tithonus eternal life, he hadn't given him eternal youth, and soon Eos found a wrinkle on Tithonus's forehead, and then a grey hair on his temple. Tithonus was getting old.

'Oh my beloved husband!' cried Eos. 'I shall go to Zeus at once, and get you made young again.' But Zeus was having another argument with Hera and would not see Eos. Weeping, she returned to Tithonus. Gradually, Tithonus got greyer and greyer, and more and more

wrinkled. His back bent, and his legs curved, and he shrank and shrank and shrank until he was so tiny he had to be kept in a little basket in case he got lost. His voice became small and shrill, and at last he turned into a tiny grasshopper, creaking his chirrupy song to his lovely wife forever more. Eos remained as young and beautiful as ever, but now the dew she sheds every morning is mixed with tears, as she mourns the loss of her handsome husband, Tithonus.

～ 23 ～

THE STARRY HUNTER

Orion was strong and brawny, with muscles like tree roots, and a beard as black as midnight. He carried a club as big as a pillar, and his jewelled sword was sharper than knives. His best friend and cousin was Artemis the huntress, and they used to run together through the woods and fields with their pack of dogs, hunting anything which came their way.

Now the king of Chios was a cunning and crafty man. His island kingdom was overrun with wild beasts, and

all his cattle and goats and sheep were being eaten up.

'If I call in Orion, and offer him my daughter in marriage, then perhaps he will rid my island of these wretched animals and I shan't have to pay him.' He meant to trick Orion into giving him something for nothing. Orion soon agreed to the bargain, because he loved to hunt, and the princess of Chios was very pretty – but what he didn't know was that she was already promised to someone else. For two weeks Orion hunted wolves and bears, lions and foxes, and at last there was not a wild beast left. He brought all the skins to the palace and laid them at the king's feet.

'The marriage will take place tomorrow,' said the crafty king. 'But now you must get some rest.' As soon as Orion had fallen asleep, the king bound him tightly with ropes, and blinded him with a hot needle. Then he dragged him down to the harbour, and threw him into

the sea. But Poseidon the sea god was Orion's father, and he sent a great wave to carry him to the east, where Helios the sun god healed his eyes. Orion strode over the waves back to Chios, but the king had seen him coming and fled with his daughter to a secret place.

Orion soon went back to hunt with Artemis on the island of Crete, and she was very pleased to see him. But Artemis' brother Apollo was jealous of his sister's friendship, so he sent a giant scorpion to attack Orion. Orion didn't hear it coming up behind him as he ran with the hunt, and its huge sting flicked out and stung

him in the heel. When Artemis turned round and found her favourite cousin dead on the ground, she was furious with her brother. But she forgave him after he helped her to shape Orion's picture in the stars. And he still hangs there in the winter heavens, his jewelled belt glittering next to his sword, the greatest hunter of them all – never to be forgotten till the world ends and the stars fall down from the sky.

24

THE DOLPHIN MESSENGER

Amphitrite lived in the underwater palace of her father, old King Nereus, together with her forty-nine beautiful sisters. Each day they rode their pet dolphins among the coral and seaweed on the bottom of the ocean, picking up pearls and precious stones that had been polished by the waves till they shone. Every evening they braided their long hair with the jewels they had found, and went to feast with their father in his great hall. Each had her own golden throne to sit on.

One night, after supper, King Nereus spoke to Amphitrite.

'My dear,' he said. 'As my eldest daughter, it is time you were getting married. I have promised you to Poseidon, the god of the sea, and I'm sure he'll make you very happy.'

Now Amphitrite was rather frightened of Poseidon since she had seen him in a temper one day. He had struck his magic trident on a rock, and made a great storm come out of nowhere, and Amphitrite had been swept onto some sharp coral and hurt her arm dreadfully.

'Oh, Father!' she cried. 'Please don't make me marry *him*!' And she ran from the hall and leapt on to her pet dolphin, whose name was Delphinus. 'Take me away and hide me!' she whispered. And Delphinus did.

When Poseidon heard that Amphitrite didn't want to marry him, he was very sad, because he truly loved her. He looked for her everywhere to try to persuade her to change her mind, but it was no good. She was too well hidden. Poseidon asked cross crabs and flickering fishes, he asked lumpy lobsters and odd octopi – he asked every creature in the sea if they had seen Amphitrite, but none of them had. So finally he went to find Delphinus.

'If you know where your mistress is, and you can persuade her to marry me, you shall have a place in the stars forever,' said Poseidon. 'I really do love her, you know.' Delphinus could see that Poseidon was telling the truth, so he took the message to Amphitrite at once.

She and Poseidon were married that day, and they

went away on their honeymoon in a chariot pulled by seven dolphins. As for Delphinus, Poseidon kept his promise, and if you look up at the sky on a clear night, you can still see him swimming among the stars.

~ 25 ~

THE BEE OF WISDOM

The great god Zeus was worried. He loved his Titan wife, Metis, because she was very clever and gave him good advice. But Mother Earth had told him that if Metis ever bore him a son, then Zeus would be overthrown. Now Zeus liked being king of the gods, and he didn't want that to happen, so he challenged Metis to a game of shape changing. Metis agreed, and as she turned into a bee and buzzed about the room, he sniffed a great sniff with his right nostril, and sucked Metis up into his head. There she sat, giving him advice when he needed it, and tickling his brain with her tiny feet when he didn't. It was rather uncomfortable, but Zeus just had to put up with it.

What Zeus didn't know was that Metis was pregnant when he turned her into a bee. Soon Metis got very bored inside Zeus's head, and she decided to make some things for her new baby. She magicked herself a loom

85

and some thread, and started to weave a beautiful robe. Thumpety-thump, clickety-click went the loom, and soon Zeus had a headache.

'Stop that!' he grumbled, but Metis carried on. As soon as she had finished the robe, she magicked herself a little hammer and anvil, and started to make a wonderful silver helmet. Bashety-bash, crashety-crash went the hammer.

'Ouch!' roared Zeus, clutching his forehead. Soon his headache was so bad that he called to his son Hephaestus the blacksmith to help him.

'Hum,' said Hephaestus. 'You've got something in there. The only thing to do is to cut it out.' So he took his sharpest chisel and split Zeus's head right open down the middle. Out sprang a beautiful goddess, wearing a shimmering silver robe and a winged silver helmet. She kissed Zeus.

'Sorry about the headache,' she said. 'I'm your daughter Athene.' As soon as Zeus had mended his head (with Metis the bee still safely inside), he invited all the gods to a feast to meet his newest daughter. He was very proud of her, and wanted to give her a present.

'I shall make her the goddess of wisdom and give her a city,' he decided. 'Perhaps that little one down there will do.'

Zeus had just chosen the one place which Poseidon

wanted to be *his* city. When Poseidon heard about Zeus's
gift to Athene he was very angry. But there was nothing
he could do to challenge his powerful brother's decision,
so he decided to challenge Athene instead.

'Let us have a competition, dear niece,' he said. 'We
shall both give the people of this place a gift, and they
shall decide which is the most useful to them. Whoever
wins shall keep the city.' Athene agreed at once, and they
both flew down to the city, landing on the flat rock the
people called the Acropolis.

'My people of Poseidia!' cried Poseidon. 'See what I
give you!' And he struck a rock with his trident. A stream
of water gushed out and the people rushed forward to
taste it.

'Ugh!' they said, spitting and coughing. 'What

horrible salty water! This is no good to us at all!'

'My people of Athens!' cried Athene. 'See what I give you!' And she pointed her finger at the ground. Up rose a beautiful tree, with silvery leaves and little hard round fruits. The fruits fell into a wooden barrel on the ground, and the people rushed to look in.

'Oh!' they cried in wonder as they scooped out oil and olives. 'How useful! How delicious! Thank you, Athene.' Poseidon dived into the sea in a fury, and ever since then, the city of Athens has belonged to the goddess Athene.

~ 26 ~

THE SHARP-EYED KING

King Sisyphus Sharp-Eyes they called him behind his back, because he never missed a thing. If there was a missing coin, Sisyphus would be sure to find it. If a child hid his toy, Sisyphus would be sure to have noticed where it was hidden. He was always stalking the streets of Corinth, watching what his people were doing, peering round corners and into windows until the people of Corinth were the best-behaved in Greece for fear that their king would catch them doing something they shouldn't.

One day, as he was walking outside the city walls, he noticed a very pretty nymph disappear into a cave followed by a cloud of shining dust.

'Aha!' he said to himself. 'That'll be Aegina running off with Zeus. I heard he was in love with her. Her father *will* be cross.' Sure enough, the next day, the river god Asopus dripped his way angrily into Sisyphus's throne room, trailing weed over the floor.

'Have you seen my daughter?' he asked. 'She's disappeared.' Sisyphus looked at Asopus and stroked his beard thoughtfully.

'I *might* know where she is,' he said. 'What's it worth?' After some hard bargaining, Asopus agreed to give Sisyphus a spring of clean water for his city, which was running dry after a drought.

'Now tell me where she is!' he growled, so Sisyphus did. Asopus ran to the cave and burst in, roaring angrily and taking his daughter and Zeus quite by surprise.

Zeus had left his thunderbolts at home, but quick as lightning he threw Aegina out of the cave door and right into the Bay of Athens.

'Become an island!' he yelled. Then he turned himself into a bit of the cave wall, so that Asopus couldn't find him.

There was a great big splash as Aegina landed in the sea. Rocks grew out of her body, and earth covered her mouth and eyes, and she spread into a small island all covered with flowers.

It took Zeus a long time to find out who had betrayed him, but when he did, King Sisyphus Sharp-Eyes was made to feel very sorry indeed that he had ever interfered with the ruler of the universe.

~ 27 ~

THE SECRET OF WINE

Semele was a mortal princess, with whom the great god Zeus fell in love. He married her secretly, hoping against hope that his jealous goddess wife, Hera, wouldn't find out. But of course she did.

Semele was six months pregnant with Zeus' baby when an old woman came to visit her, carrying a large basket.

'Rattles and toys!' she croaked. 'Rattles and toys! Buy my pretty rattles and toys!' Semele was delighted and bought several for when the new baby arrived.

'But where is your husband, my dear?' asked the old woman slyly.

'My husband is the great god Zeus himself. He's too busy doing important things and ruling the world to be here all the time,' said Semele proudly. But the old woman didn't seem to believe her.

'Does he glow in the dark? Have you ever

seen his thunder-bolts?
How do you *know*?' she
asked. 'You should ask
him to prove it, just in
case he's lying!' Then she
went away and as soon as
she was outside the palace,
she turned back into Hera
and flew up to Olympus.

Well, Semele lay
awake all that night,
wondering and won-
dering, and the next
time Zeus came to
visit, she begged
and begged him to
show her just one
thunder-bolt.

'Just to prove you
really are Zeus,' she
said, fluttering her
eyelashes. Zeus took
the smallest thunder-
bolt out from his bag,
but it sizzled so
scorchingly that it
burnt   poor
Semele

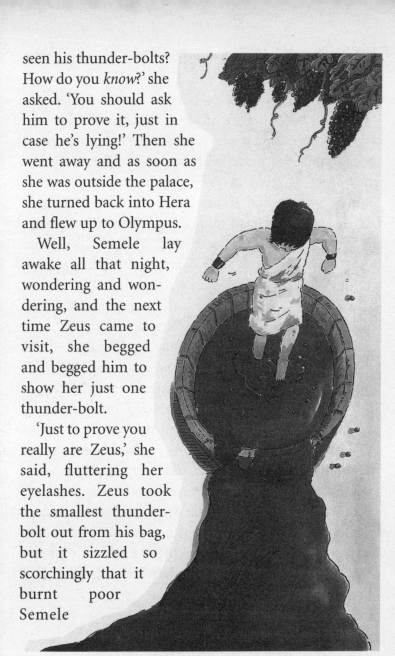

to death. Zeus only just had time to save the baby, which he sewed under the skin of his right thigh.

As soon as Dionysius was born, Zeus hid him away in a beautiful valley, where he grew up with the Maenads, wild dancing maidens who gave wonderful parties for all the nymphs and fauns and satyrs. All over the valley grew vines, covered in juicy purple grapes. One day, Dionysius was bored, so he tipped a lot of grapes into a barrel and started to dance on them. The grapes  squelched under his feet, and soon a lot of juice appeared. Dionysius scooped it into a cup, meaning to drink it, but the Maenads called him to a party, and he forgot all about it. Two weeks later, a delicious smell wafted from the cup as Dionysius walked past. He ran over and drank it down, and that was how wine was invented.

Dionysius went all over the world teaching humans to make this wonderful drink, and everywhere he went, people worshipped him as a new god. Zeus was very proud of him, and even Hera, when she had tried some wine, admitted that it was as nice as ambrosia, and even nicer than nectar. She and Zeus threw a party for him on Olympus, and there he was given his official title – Dionysius, god of wine.

RAINBOW EGGS

The queen of Sparta hung her robe on a bush and dived into the stream. The water was icy cold, but Leda sang as she washed herself. Today something good was going to happen, she could just feel it.

At that very moment Zeus sailed by on a cloud and looked down. He saw Leda's perfect pearly arms raised above her head as she dived, and fell in love at once. Quickly he summoned Aphrodite. She was very sympathetic – love was her business, after all.

'If I turn into a hawk, and you turn into a swan, I can chase you into Leda's arms,' she said. 'I know she loves birds, and she won't be able to resist stroking your soft white feathers.'

The swan flapped frantically up the stream towards Leda with the hawk swooping at its tail.

'Oh! You poor thing!' cried Leda. 'I'll protect you. Shoo! Shoo! You horrible hawk!' The hawk swerved away as Leda flapped her hands at it, and the swan nestled into her arms. 'What a beautiful creature you are,' she said, smoothing its ruffled feathers and kissing the top of its elegant head. 'Why, I'm quite in love with you already!'

Nine months later, Leda produced two beautiful eggs. The first shone with bright rainbow colours, and out of it came the lovely Helen of Sparta, who later caused so much trouble to the Greeks and Trojans, and her sister Clytemnestra. The second had a pattern of swirling silver mist, and out of it came the twin brothers Castor and Polydeuces, who became famous heroes. When they died, Zeus took them up to the heavens and made them into twin stars, where they still shine today, hand in hand.

Although she loved all her children very much, Leda was *most* surprised to have laid a pair of eggs, and she vowed never to have anything to do with birds again for the rest of her life.

~ 29 ~

WAR AND STRIFE

The clash of swords and the screams of fighting men rose up to Olympus from earth, and drifted in at the window of the palace of war. Ares, the god of war, was asleep, but as soon as he heard the commotion he leapt off his couch and shook his companion Eris, the spirit of strife. Eris had a golden apple which was so beautiful that everyone wanted to own it. It caused a lot of arguments, which pleased Eris very much – the more arguments the better as far as she was concerned.

'Come on, Eris!' yelled Ares, strapping on his sword as he ran. 'Into the battle chariot, quick!' Eris grabbed her helmet and jammed it down over her spiky black hair. She had mean green eyes and a thin sneering mouth which only smiled when her friends Pain, Hunger and Desperation played a nasty joke on some poor human.

Ares's battle chariot had just enough room for two people. Its wheels were armed with dangerous pointed spikes, and the black horses which drew it wore silver

97

armour and had teeth as sharp as daggers. It swept down
to earth and hovered above the battle. Ares and Eris
yelled gleeful encouragement to both sides, and soon
they were in the thick of the fighting themselves.
Suddenly a tall soldier with a yellow plume in his helmet

came up behind Ares and stabbed him in the calf. All at once Ares began to cry.

'Oh! Oh! Oh! it hurts!' he sobbed. 'Someone get me a bandage! Oh! Oh! Oh! I'm going to die!' Now of course gods can't die, because they are immortal and live forever. Ares knew this perfectly well. But he always made a terrible fuss when he was wounded, because he was a dreadful coward at heart.

Eris took Ares back to Olympus, where Zeus gave him some magic ointment and his wound healed immediately.

'Now go away and don't come back!' said Zeus crossly. He disliked Ares because he was so vain and boastful as well as being a coward.

That night Ares gave a feast for all his friends. He sat on his golden throne and boasted about how brave he had been that day, and they all cheered and applauded. But Eris just sat beside him and fingered her beautiful golden apple, and wondered whom it would be nice to upset next.

~ 30 ~

THE BABY AND
THE COWS

Maia was the smallest of the Titans. She was always laughing and dancing and picking flowers, and all the gods were very fond of her. But the one who loved her most was Zeus. They married in secret, and because Maia lived in a deep, dark cave on faraway Mount Cyllene, jealous Hera never found out. In due course Maia had a little son, whom she called Hermes. Like his mother, he loved to laugh, and a cheerier, chubbier, cuddlier baby could not have been found anywhere. He was also very clever and loved to play tricks and jokes on his fellow gods. Almost as soon as he was born he sneaked out of his cradle and ran on his baby feet out of the cave and all the way to the Arcadian Meadows, where his brother Apollo's precious white cows were grazing on the soft green grass. Apollo was lying quietly under a tree, singing a little song and dozing in the hot sun.

'Hec hee!' Hermes giggled. 'Won't Apollo be surprised when his best cows disappear without leaving any tracks! He'll think a monster has eaten them!' He tiptoed through the flowers and rounded up the fifty fattest cows.

'Quiet!' he whispered as he bound up their hooves with birch bark, and tied straw brooms to their tails so that they would sweep away their own hoofprints. 'Come with me!'

On the way home to Maia's cave Hermes felt a bit hungry, so he sat down and ate two whole cows. Then he took the long curvy horns and some other bits of the cows he had eaten, and made a lyre. It was the first lyre ever made in the world, and Hermes was rather pleased with it.

Soon he had hidden the cows in a wood and sneaked back to his cradle, where he snuggled down for a nap.

'You naughty baby!' whispered Maia from her bed. 'Where on earth have you been?' But Hermes just burped contentedly. He *had* eaten rather a lot of cow, after all.

At dawn Apollo came raging and shouting into the cave. 'Where are my cows?' he yelled. 'I know you stole them!' But Hermes just gurgled happily.

Apollo turned scarlet.

'Don't you goo at me, you – you – BABY!' And he scooped him up and whisked him straight up to Olympus, where he burst in on an important meeting of the gods. 'This – this – INFANT has stolen my lovely cows, and he won't tell me where they are!' The gods looked startled for a moment, then they burst out laughing. They laughed until they were rolling about on the floor. Little baby Hermes looked so funny standing beside big tall Apollo.

'Oh dear!' said Zeus, wiping the tears from his eyes. 'I suppose you'd better have them back. Show your brother where they are, you bad baby!' And Hermes had to do what Zeus said. On the way he picked up his new lyre and showed it to his brother. He ran his fat little fingers across the strings, and a shower of silvery notes pealed out and rang around the valleys.

Now Apollo liked music even more than cows, and the lyre was the most wonderful instrument he had ever heard. In the end

Hermes got all the cows as well as Apollo's magic staff, just so Apollo could have the lyre all to himself. And Zeus was so proud of his baby son that he made him the messenger of the gods, and gave him a pair

of winged sandals, a magical winged hat and a cloak of invisibility, so that he could flit about the world unseen.

Hermes never stole again, but the gods and goddesses on Olympus always kept a careful eye out for the clever tricks and jokes he played on them every single day.

THE KING WHO
TRICKED DEATH

Zeus was very cross with King Sisyphus Sharp-Eyes for getting him into trouble.

'Hades,' he said to his gloomy brother. 'I want you to drag that wretched king's soul down to your darkest pit, and leave it there for a very long time.' So Hades went off to Corinth to do as his brother had asked. Sisyphus pretended to be delighted when Hades arrived.

'How lovely to see you, dear Hades,' said Sisyphus. 'But why are you here? If you want to take my soul down to your kingdom of Tartarus, you really should have sent Hermes along. It is his job to take souls to the Underworld after all.'

Now Sisyphus was perfectly right, and Hades knew it. While he was thinking what to do, Sisyphus whipped a strong chain around his chest and tied him to a large pillar in the courtyard.

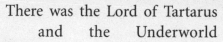

There was the Lord of Tartarus and the Underworld trussed up like a chicken. Hades was very angry, but there was nothing he could do. None of the mortals could die properly while he was tied up, and so the whole world ran around bumping into the souls which should have been taken down to the Underworld. It was all a dreadful muddle, but in the end the gods forced Sisyphus to untie Hades and let him go.

Hades didn't make the same mistake twice, and as soon as he was safely down in Tartarus, he sent Hermes to take Sisyphus's soul. But sneaky Sisyphus had dressed up as a beggar, and told his wife not to give him a funeral feast, nor to put a coin under his tongue when he died.

When he and Hermes arrived at the river Styx, he couldn't pay the old boatman to take him across.

'Sorry, Charon,' he said. 'No money.' So Hermes had to take him round the long beggar's way. Hades was even angrier than before when they arrived. The rules said that no king could come into the Underworld without a magnificent funeral feast and a golden coin under his tongue. Sisyphus had neither.

'What a terrible wife you have,' raged Hades. 'You must go back to Corinth at once and teach her how to behave. Really! What a dreadful example she is setting to all the other kings' wives. I shall have no gold coming down here at all at this rate!' So Sisyphus went happily back to Corinth, and kissed his wife as soon as he got there.

'Well done, dear,' he said. 'We tricked them nicely!'

Sisyphus died of old age after many happy years with his beloved wife. But Hades had his revenge in the end. When Sisyphus finally got down to Tartarus, he gave him a huge boulder.

'Push that up a hill,' he snarled. And so poor Sisyphus had to push. Every time he reached the top of the hill, the boulder rolled down, and he had to start all over again. He never did reach the top, and he may well be pushing that boulder still.

~ 32 ~

THE HUNDRED-EYED WATCHMAN

The goddess Hera was sure her husband Zeus was up to something. He had been acting strangely all week, and now she wanted to find out why.

Below on earth it was a beautiful calm sunny day, and as Hera peered suspiciously down from Olympus, she saw a funny thing. A black cloud was moving mysteriously fast along the ground, wriggling and shaking as if something was inside it. Hera dived straight into the middle of the cloud to see if she could catch Zeus with yet another nymph. But when she landed, Zeus was standing there quite innocently, stroking the head of a pretty white cow with a golden halter round her neck.

'My dove!' he said, smiling at Hera nervously. 'How nice of you to drop in!' Hera smiled back, but it was a smile full of danger. She knew perfectly

107

well that the cow had been a nymph seconds before. She held out her hand.

'Give her to me at once,' she commanded. So Zeus gave her the cow. Hera took the cow – whose name was Io – straight to the secret garden which Gaia had given her as a wedding present, and tied her to a tree. Poor Io mooed miserably as Hera set Argus, the monster with a hundred never-sleeping eyes, to guard her. She didn't like being a cow at all!

Zeus didn't dare rescue Io himself, so he asked his son Hermes to try.

'She keeps me awake at night with her mooing, and besides, it's not her fault that Hera's so jealous.' So off went Hermes, wearing a shepherd's tunic, and he skipped right up to Argus and tootled at him on his flute.

'Hello, old monster!' he said. 'Still keeping a few eyes on things, I see.' Argus grunted. He found being a watchman very dull. It wasn't like fighting other monsters at all. Argus was good at fighting monsters – in fact he had fought the dreadful Echidna, one of the two hideous creatures made long ago by Mother Earth, and killed her.

Hermes began to play a funny little tune on his flute. It was drowsy and dozy and sleepy, and very boring. Soon Argus's eyes began to close. First one, then ten, then fifty, then all hundred eyes snapped shut. Hermes tapped each eye with his magic staff, and Argus fell over dead. Quickly Hermes untied Io, but as soon as she was free she ran home to her father, the river god Inachus. He recognised her at once, even though she was a cow, and rushed off in a fury to kill Zeus. But Zeus saw him coming, and threw a thunderbolt at him.

When Hera discovered that Argus was dead, she wept and wailed. She took his hundred eyes, and stuck them to the tail of her favourite peacock, and there they sit to this day. Then she sent a huge buzzing gadfly after Io. It chased her all over Greece, biting and stinging her till she ran all the way to Egypt. There Hera allowed Zeus to turn her back into a nymph, and the Egyptians worshipped her as a goddess. But Hera made Zeus swear a solemn promise that he would never try to see Io again.

~ 33 ~

THE HUNTRESS
IN THE POOL

Artemis the huntress stood polishing her great silver bow, while Zeus looked on proudly.

'What was it you wanted me for, dear daughter?' he asked.

'Just a little thing, father,' said Artemis. 'I love my life in the woods and I love to be free, so please, dear, dear Zeus, don't ever make me marry anyone.' Zeus was rather startled, but he wanted to please his daughter so he agreed.

'I shall give you a golden chariot, fifty nymphs to guard you, and a pack of my best hounds, so you may run free through the woods forever.'

'Thank you,' said Artemis, kissing him on the forehead.

Artemis had a lovely time hunting the deer and the wild boar with her nymphs and her lollopy loppy-eared lemon-spotted hounds. At first the nymphs pulled her chariot themselves, but then Artemis captured four of the five magical hinds who lived on the slopes of Mount Ceryneia, and she trained them to pull the chariot instead. Sometimes Artemis was joined by her best friend Orion, but most of the time she hunted alone.

One evening, when the moon was hanging heavy and golden in the sky, a brave young hunter called Actaeon set out with his pack of hounds to chase a great white stag which he had heard was loose in the forest. Soon the hounds were belling and baying and barking through the woods, with Actaeon hard on their heels. All at once he crashed into a clearing. The moonlight shone on the pool in the middle where a beautiful maiden was bathing. A pack of lemon-yellow spotted hounds sat on the bank behind her, growling. Actaeon stood and stared with his mouth open in amazement.

'Wretched hunter!' shouted the maiden. 'How dare you interrupt my bath. No man may see the goddess Artemis bare!' And she scooped up some water and flung it at Actaeon's head. As soon as the drops started to run down his cheeks, Actaeon felt some-

thing strange happening to him. His body thickened and became covered in coarse white hair, his arms and legs lengthened and grew hooves, and his head sprouted a pair of magnificent antlers. Actaeon the stag lifted his head and roared with anguish, as his own hounds leapt on him and tore him to pieces.

'He did make a beautiful stag, but he shouldn't have looked,' said Artemis, climbing out to dry herself, as she patted his hounds gently. Afterwards she took them into her own pack, and when they died, she sent them to hunt with Orion among the stars.

THE CLOTH OF LIFE

In the time before time, Nyx the goddess of Night spread her great cloak around the universe and held it close.

'Hush!' she sang. 'Sleep!' And the universe slept. Deep inside Nyx grew three stars, and the stars became powerful and strong. Soon they were stronger than their mother, and they commanded that she should unwrap the universe and share it with Day. Nyx agreed. But as she unwrapped her cloak, 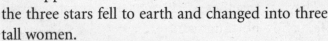 the three stars fell to earth and changed into three tall women.

The first was a young maiden.

'I shall spin the threads of life,' she sang as she twirled her spindle. 'I shall spin the red thread of anger and the blue thread of calm, the white thread of peace and joy and the black thread of despair.' And she set to work at once.

The second was a beautiful woman.

'I shall decide the length of the threads of life,' she

sang as she took out a measuring tape. 'I shall measure up heroes who live short lives and cowards who live long. I shall decide when death will come knocking on the doors of kings and commoners, priests and princes, beggars and basketmakers.' And she set to work at once.

The third was an old, withered crone.

'I shall cut the threads of life,' she sang as she opened a great pair of shears. 'I shall snip the lives of all men and women, old and young, rich or poor. My scissors will cut every thread when the time is right.' And she set to work at once.

The three women came to be known to men and gods as the Fates. They sat together working at their great tapestry of life, and nothing and nobody could persuade them to change or move a single thread. Although the gods gave them precious gifts and men and women prayed to them every day for the life of a child or a loved one, their power was so great that they

just went on spinning and measuring and snipping without ever once taking any notice. Their tapestry grew and grew and became more and more complicated as time went by. And it will go on growing till the world ends and Nyx's cloak covers the universe once more.

~ 35 ~

THE KINDLY ONES

When the Titan, Cronus, gave his father Uranus the great wound that sent him running into the outer darkness of heaven, four drops of Uranus's blood fell to earth. One drop fell into the sea and became the goddess Aphrodite, but the other three drops soaked into the rich soil that lay around Mount Cronus. Soon three small mounds appeared. The earth boiled and bubbled around them, until, *pop pop pop*, hundreds of snakes' heads came out of each mound. Finally three fierce-looking women pushed their way out of the heaving soil. Each had snakes instead of hair, a large pair of copper-coloured wings, a whip in the left hand, and a blazing torch in the right.

'Furies!' they cried harshly as they emerged. 'We are the Furies!' Then they started to flap their huge wings and sniff about with their long pointed noses, as the snakes on their heads hissed and wriggled.

'We will light up the hiding places of the wicked ones with our bright torches. We will whip them to the ends of the earth and punish them!' they chanted. And with a great whoosh of coppery feathers they rose into the air and flew off into the world.

For many years the Furies chased and killed those who were unlucky enough or stupid enough to break their laws, and sometimes they made mistakes. But eventually Apollo and Athene, who were tired of the bloodshed, persuaded them to put down their torches and whips, and gave them a temple to themselves. There they became known as the Kindly Ones, and the people were so thankful to be saved from their terrible punishments, that they gave them presents and sacrifices forever after.

~ 36 ~

THE GAMES
OF THE GODS

It was a very dangerous thing to be in love with Princess Hippodamia of Elis. Her father, King Oenomaus, had ordered that anyone who wanted to marry her must first race against the team of magic horses which had been given to him by Ares, the cowardly god of war. If the suitor won, the wedding would take place at once. But if he lost, King Oenomaus would chop his head off.

Pelops (the same one who was put in a stew by his father, Tantalus) had heard of Hippodamia's beauty, and he decided to try his luck. He set off with his own team of magical horses, which had been given to him by the gods to make up for being chopped up and served at a feast by his own father.

'After all my horses came from Zeus himself, so they must be able to beat a team that was given by a

coward like Ares,' he said to himself.

As soon as he saw Hippodamia Pelops fell in love with her and she with him. But Hippodamia didn't know that Pelops had a team of magic horses too. So she bribed a stable boy to loosen a nut on one of her father's chariot wheels, so that it would wobble and go slowly. She wanted Pelops to win. The stable boy hated King Oenomaus, because his elder brother had been one of Hippodamia's unsuccessful suitors, and had had his head chopped off by the king. So instead of loosening just one nut, he took them all out, and replaced them with wax ones.

'Serve him right if he dies!' he thought with a nasty grin.

The red flag dipped, and the horses raced off. At first they were evenly matched, and the chariots hurtled neck and neck round the course. But soon Pelops began to draw ahead, and King Oenomaus's chariot began to wobble as the wax nuts melted. There was an earsplitting screech of metal as the chariot flew apart, and the king was thrown to the ground. As Pelops drew up, Hippodamia began to cry and to shake the stable boy, who was standing beside her.

'Wretched wretch! I only asked you to loosen a little nut, so my beloved Pelops would win. Now my father is dead!' she wailed. The stable boy wriggled out of her grip and ran backwards through the crowd, but Pelops strode forward and seized him. Then he marched him to the nearest cliff and threw him into the sea.

'Before I marry Hippodamia, we shall have a fabulous funeral feast for her father!' he declared. 'We shall invite all the kings and heroes, and afterwards we shall hold games at Olympia, with prizes of gold and jewels for the winners.'

The gods themselves looked down on the games and declared them to be such a success that after Pelops and Hippodamia were married they announced that they would hold them every four years. And so the Olympic Games were created for heroes and heroines from all over Greece to prove their strength and their skill to gods and mortals alike.

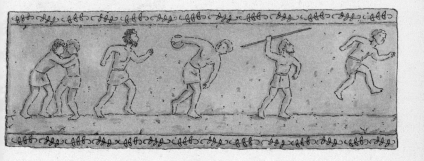

~ 37 ~

THE STRONGEST MAN

There was simply no one stronger than Heracles. He was the son of Zeus and the Princess Alcmene, and the great-grandson of Perseus who had killed Medusa the Gorgon. Even when he was a baby he was so strong that he strangled the two huge spotted snakes the goddess Hera had sent to bite him in his cradle. She hated him because her husband Zeus had run off with his mother.

Heracles' enormous strength meant he was not an easy child to have around a polite palace where people behaved themselves, and didn't run around roaring and shouting and breaking things. When he was learning the lyre, his huge fingers plucked the strings so hard that they broke. When he sang, his great voice cracked and broke on the high notes. In fact Heracles hated singing so much that one day he gave his teacher what he thought was a tiny tap with

the lyre, and killed him stone dead. After that he was sent away to be a shepherd.

Heracles was much happier in the mountains, where he could wrestle with lions and bears and wolves to his heart's content. Soon stories of his deeds spread all the way to Thebes, where even King Creon heard of them.

'I must have this hero for my son-in-law!' he said, and he summoned Heracles to come and marry his daughter Megara. Heracles and Megara were happy together, and soon they had lots of children. Heracles loved them all and used to bring them lion cubs to play with. But one day Hera looked down from Olympus and saw Heracles laughing.

'I'll teach him to laugh!' she muttered, and she sent a horrible black cloud of madness to attack Heracles. As soon as it touched him, he imagined he was surrounded by wild beasts, so he killed them all. When the cloud drifted back to Olympus he discovered that Megara and all his children were dead.

'What shall I do?' he wailed, tearing his hair and beating his great chest.

'You must go to Delphi and ask Apollo's oracle for advice,' said King Creon, tears running down into his beard. So Heracles went to Delphi to learn what he must do to make up for the awful crime he had committed.

Now the King of Tiryns at that time was Eurystheus, who was Heracles' cousin. He was jealous of Heracles, because he himself was weak and puny, with arms like sticks, thin yellow legs and a squeaky voice. When he heard that the oracle had ordered Heracles to serve him for ten years, and do ten difficult tasks for him, he was delighted. Hera was pleased too, because Eurystheus was a friend of hers, and she knew she could help him to think up some impossible things for Heracles to do.

So Heracles came to the gates of Tiryns to report to his cousin for orders. For the next ten years he had to do everything that Eurystheus said, but he didn't mind at all. He just hoped that one day he would be able to forget the terrible terrible thing he had done.

~ 38 ~

CATTLE STEALER

King Eurystheus had set Heracles an impossible task. He rubbed his hands gleefully as he summoned his cousin to the throne room.

'I want those nice fat red cows belonging to Geryon,' he squeaked. 'And I want them in a year and a day!' Heracles sighed. He would have to hurry. Geryon's island was at the farthest edge of the Western Ocean, and a year and a day wasn't nearly long enough to get there and back. He ran to the edge of the land and dived into the sea. Soon he was swimming strongly westwards. But even after he had swum a long long way, Geryon's island was still not in sight, and Heracles was getting tired. He turned over on his back for a rest, and looked up into the sky. Sailing just above him was Helios the sun god in his golden cloud boat. Heracles swam to the nearest rock and hauled himself out of the water. Fitting a huge arrow to his bow, he took aim and shouted:

'Hey, Helios! Lend me your boat for a bit or I'll shoot you down!' Helios had no choice, so he steered his boat to the rock, and got out crossly, pulling his chariot and horses behind him.

'I'll need it back,' he said sulkily. 'And mind you don't

bump it on anything.' Heracles pulled two great craggy boulders off the rock and threw them into the ocean so that he could find his way home. They stuck up above the waves, and sailors in later times called them the Pillars of Heracles. Then he set the sails, and vanished into the west.

At last he saw a huge island in front of him. It was covered in flat grassy plains, on which several herds of fat red cattle were grazing. Heracles landed the boat quietly, and sneaked ashore. As soon as he had set foot on land, a huge two-headed dog rushed at him barking. Heracles wrestled it to the ground and threw it into a bush. He set out towards the cattle, but before he could reach them, he was attacked by a hideous giant who was Geryon's shepherd. Heracles punched him in the head and knocked him over. Then he dragged him over to a water-hole and pushed him into it. Heracles was just rounding up the last cow when he heard a great roar.

Geryon himself was running out from his palace.

'How dare you steal my cattle!' he cried, spit and foam flying from his three mouths. Heracles calmly fixed three arrows to his bow, and shot Geryon in each of his three bodies. *Pluff pluff pluff* went the arrows, and Geryon's spindly legs wobbled as he sank to the ground, quite dead.

The red cattle walked quietly into the boat and Heracles sailed back to the mainland. It took him a long time, as the boat didn't like going the wrong way round the world. Just as he was giving the boat back to Helios, Hera sent a cloud of her most vicious gadflies to sting the cows, and they scattered everywhere. Heracles only just had time to round them up on the last day of the year. He drove them to the gates of Tiryns before dawn the next day and yelled up at the windows.

'Cousin Eurystheus! Here are your cows! I've finished my task!' Eurystheus looked out smiling unpleasantly.

Heracles might think he'd finished, but he and Hera had another couple of things for him to do before he was free.

'Oh Heracles! Come here a minute!' he called. And poor Heracles trudged into the throne room once again to hear what his next task was to be.

~ 39 ~

THE DIRTIEST JOB
IN THE WORLD

King Eurystheus of Tiryns had just set his cousin Heracles another terrible task. He had got together with the goddess Hera to think of something *really* difficult this time, and he rubbed his hands gleefully at the thought of Heracles' face when he had heard what he had to do.

'A little bit of dirt will do him good,' he chuckled.

Augeias, King of Elis, had three hundred black bulls and two hundred red, as well as twelve silver and white bulls which were sacred to the gods. He also had herds and herds of wonderful cows. Their mooing kept everyone in Elis awake far into the night, and the clouds of their breath shut out the early morning sun. Their barnyards and stables were filled with dung to the height of five men, and they hadn't been cleaned out for twenty years. The smell was truly dreadful, and the people of Elis all wore masks over their noses.

Heracles only had a year to clean the stables and barns, and to make the floors spotless enough for King Augeias to eat his dinner off. It certainly was an impossible task.

But Heracles was not going to be beaten by a bit of muck. He sat in the middle of a herd of black and red cows, scratching his head and thinking hard. Suddenly he heard the sound of rushing water, and then he had an idea. Elis was built between two rivers. If he could only persuade the rivers to flow through the barns and stables, they would be clean in no time at all. And best of all, he could just sit and watch.

Heracles worked hard to persuade the two rivers to move out of their courses, but at last he managed. 'It's only for a day,' he said to the river gods, herding the cattle carefully on to a nearby hill.

Next morning King Augeias and the people of Elis saw a wonderful sight. Two great walls of green water were swirling through the mountains of muck, and washing it away to the sea. Soon the stables and barns were as shining and clean as a spring morning, and that night King Augeias ordered a celebration feast.

'I shall eat it off the stable floor!' he laughed, and he invited Heracles to join him.

When Eurystheus heard of Heracles' success, he flung his crown on the ground and jumped on it. 'I'll get him yet!' he vowed crossly as he went to think up another impossible task.

~ 40 ~

THE BIGGEST PIG

'Come here, Heracles,' said King Eurystheus. 'I've thought up another task. My people tell me that a huge and horrible boar is roaming through the countryside up by Mount Erymanthus. It's as big as a house, and it has tusks as long as lances and sharper than scissors. It's killing everything it sees, and it seems to be rather fierce. I want you to go and catch it for me. And mind you bring it back alive.'

Heracles gathered his weapons and wrapped himself up warmly. It was winter, and snow was falling softly as he slipped out of the palace gates. He was rather looking forward to this task, although he was more used to killing boar than capturing them. It took him a long time to get to Mount Erymanthus, but at last he arrived, and he walked around the snowy mountain, thinking out his plan.

Suddenly he heard crashing and grunting above him, and the enormous boar appeared out of the bushes, and ran into a large cave. His little piggy eyes were flashing red with fury, and his tusks were dripping with blood and foam. The bristles on his back stood up like needles, and he was at least as big as a house, if not bigger.

'Ho! Boar!' shouted Heracles. 'Come and fight me if you dare!' There was a squeal of rage, and the boar charged out of the cave again. But Heracles was too clever for him. He ran off up the mountain like a hare, and the boar galloped behind him. The snow got deeper and deeper, and soon the heavy boar was exhausted. His body sank into the snow and stuck fast in a snowdrift. Quickly, Heracles bundled him into a strong chain net, and then he carried him on his shoulders all the way to the gates of Tiryns.

'Cousin Eurystheus!' he called. 'I've got the boar you wanted!' But when Eurystheus saw the sharp tusks and heard the great animal squealing and raging to get at him, he ran inside and hid himself in a large bronze jar which he had ordered to be made. Unfortunately one of his servants had filled it with olive oil. And oh! weren't his best robes sticky and greasy when he finally dared to climb out!

THE GOLDEN DEER

Artemis had four magical golden hinds which she used to pull her hunting chariot. But their sister was even more beautiful. She had been too fast even for Artemis to catch, and so she lived in the woods, where Artemis declared her sacred and under her protection.

King Eurystheus had heard about the famous hind from Hera, and he knew how much it would annoy Artemis if she were caught.

'If I tell Heracles to bring me the hind,' he thought, 'he will never dare to offend Artemis, and so he will fail. Then I can punish him.' He summoned Heracles at once.

'Go to Ceryneia, and bring me Artemis' golden deer,' he said. 'She will be a nice ornament for the palace gardens.'

Heracles went straight to Ceryneia and hid by a pool in the woods. Sure enough the golden deer stepped out of the trees in the evening light and started to drink. Her coat was like sunshine, and her horns shone like fire. As Heracles started to chase after her, her hooves flashed bronze lightning, and she ran faster than the wind. Heracles chased the golden deer for a whole year from Istria to the land of Tauris, but eventually she sank down, exhausted, and Heracles tied her feet together and carried her back to his cousin in Tiryns.

'How pretty she is,' said King Eurystheus as

he stroked her soft ears and released her among his flowerbeds.

The golden hind only stayed for two days in Eurystheus's palace gardens. Then she jumped over the wall and ran back to the woods of Ceryneia, where she has lived happily ever since.

~ 42 ~

FIRE BREATHER

King Minos of Crete had a problem. A gigantic bull was rampaging all over his island, rooting up the trees with his enormous horns, and trampling the crops with his huge feet.

'I need a hero to deal with this animal,' he said to himself. 'I wonder if my friend Eurystheus would lend me Heracles.'

Eurystheus was delighted. He needed another task for Heracles, and this one sounded perfect. 'Bring the bull back here at once,' he commanded. 'I can use it against my enemies. It will be better than a whole army!'

When Heracles arrived in Minos's wonderful palace, the king was in the middle of a feast. He was very pleased to see Heracles.

'Sit down! Try some of these larks' wings – or perhaps a little simmered turtle egg.' Just then a messenger ran in.

'Your Majesty!' he said, bowing and panting. 'The citizens of Cydonia are terrified. The bull has driven them all into one house, and he's stamping and snorting and breathing fire from his nostrils. They are trapped!'

Heracles leapt up.

'No time for feasting, your Majesty,' he said. 'I'll be off!' And he grabbed his weapons and followed the messenger out of the door.

The streets of Cydonia were deserted, but from the end of the city came a dreadful screaming and wailing, together with a loud thudding sound. As Heracles ran up, the bull was charging at the door of a large house. His fiery breath had set all the grass alight, and men and women and children were hanging out of the windows, throwing water at it with buckets drawn from the well in the courtyard.

Heracles took a deep breath and bellowed. The bull turned round at once. His little eyes turned scarlet with rage, and sparks flew from his giant hooves. Heracles held out his arms, and as the bull charged at him, he somersaulted on to its back. The bull was very surprised indeed! It ran around the whole island of Crete, trying to throw Heracles off. But Heracles held on with all his might, and squeezed the bull's ribs with his strong legs until it had no breath left, and collapsed on the ground exhausted. Heracles threw a strong iron chain around its neck, and made it swim behind his boat all the way to the mainland. Then he dragged it back to Tiryns, right into the throne room. When the bull could breathe again, it started to bellow.

'Take it to Hera's temple!' squeaked King Eurystheus, quickly hopping into the safety of his bronze jar again. 'I give it to her as a gift.' But Hera didn't want the bull, so she sent it running all over Greece, until it was so tired that it lay down and died.

Heracles went and looked into the jar. 'So, little cousin,' he asked. 'What would you like me to bring you next?'

~ 43 ~

THE MAN–EATING MARES

Now that Heracles had succeeded in so many of the tasks he had been given by his cousin, King Eurystheus, he was feeling quite confident. But the goddess Hera was furious.

'You haven't given him anything difficult enough!' she screeched at the terrified king as he cowered in his bronze jar. 'Heracles must fail, and then I shall have an excuse to punish him. All these successes are making his head even bigger than it was before!'

Eurystheus nodded. 'I know, great Queen of Heaven,' he said. 'But he's just so *good* at everything.' Then Hera leaned over and whispered in his ear. Eurystheus began to laugh. 'Perfect!' he sniggered, as he called for Heracles to attend him at once.

Hera had told Eurystheus to send Heracles to capture the four mares belonging to King Diomedes of Thrace. Heracles didn't like horses very much – other animals were all right, but horses kicked and bit, and these mares were particularly nasty. Whenever King Diomedes had strangers as guests, he would treat them to a feast, and if anyone had too much wine and got drunk he would chop them up and feed them to his horses. The mares had got used to eating human flesh, and every time a new groom came near them, they would crunch great lumps out of him with their sharp teeth.

Heracles sailed to Thrace, and when he landed, he tied up his boat and went boldly up to the king's palace. When King Diomedes saw this fine-looking stranger, he smiled a wicked smile.

'A huge man like that will feed my horses for a week!' he thought, as he gave orders for a feast to be prepared, and invited Heracles to join him. Diomedes poured cup after cup of wine for Heracles, but Heracles secretly tipped them behind the silk cushions without anyone noticing. Soon he pretended to go to sleep, and snored loudly. When he felt King Diomedes start to tie up his arms and legs, he leapt up.

'Wretched king!' he roared, brandishing his club. 'You shall suffer the same fate you intended for me!' And whacking the king on the head he lifted him up, and threw him into the brass manger in the mares' stable. The four horses gobbled the king up right away, but as soon as they finished the last mouthful, they became calm and docile, and allowed Heracles to put on their golden bridles and lead them away to his boat.

'Your man-eating horses, dear cousin,' he said as they trotted behind him into Eurystheus's throne room. The horses licked their lips and looked at Eurystheus hungrily.

'L-lock th-them in the s-s-tables,' stuttered Eurystheus from the safety of his bronze jar. And up on Olympus, Hera looked down and gnashed her teeth in rage as she saw that Heracles had succeeded once again in completing an impossible task.

~ 44 ~

THE MAGIC SKIN

The very first task that Heracles ever had to perform for King Eurystheus was to kill the Nemean lion. This lion was one of the children of the terrible monsters Echidna and Typhon, and it was a most dreadful beast.

Heracles met no one on his way to Nemea – the lion had devoured them all – so he had to search for a long time before he found the lion's cave. When he did find it, the lion was just returning after a day's hunting. He was covered in blood, and flies were buzzing after him as he padded along on his huge paws, swishing his tail like a cat. Heracles hid in a bush and shot several sharp arrows at him. But to his surprise the arrows bounced off, and the lion just yawned and lay down to sleep off his meal. Heracles yelled and

143

charged at him with his sword. It was the strongest sword ever made, but the lion's hide was so tough that it just bent and broke as if it was made of wax. The lion didn't even wake up.

Heracles only had one weapon left – the twisted, knotted club he had had as a boy for protecting his sheep. It was covered in sharp metal spikes, and Heracles lifted it over his shoulders and brought it smashing down on the lion's head. The lion growled and shook his head a little because his ears were ringing, and then he retired into the cave to finish his interrupted sleep.

Heracles looked at the splintered piece of wood in his hands. Whatever could he do? The lion couldn't be killed with any weapon, that was obvious. Heracles would just have to rely on his own strength. He ran into the cave and jumped onto the sleeping lion's back. He put his huge hands round the lion's neck and began to squeeze. At this, the lion woke up, and began to thrash and roar and roll around the cave floor. But Heracles didn't let go until he was dead.

The people of Tiryns gasped as they saw the lion draped round Heracles' neck. He walked straight into the throne room, and dumped the dead animal at Eurystheus's feet.

'Ugh!' shrieked Eurystheus, running behind a curtain. 'Take it away.' So Heracles took it away and skinned it with its own sharp claws, and made the skin into armour, which nothing could penetrate. He made the head into a helmet, which he wore whenever he went into battle.

It was after this that the cowardly Eurystheus ordered a great bronze jar to be made, and he decided to hide in it if ever Heracles should bring such a fearsome beast near him again.

~ 45 ~
THE GOLDEN APPLES

Heracles had finished his tasks in exactly eight years and a month.

'Can I go now?' he asked. Eurystheus smiled nastily.

'Oh, I don't think so. Not just yet,' he said. 'Hera says you ought to do two more things for me, because Iolaus helped you with the Hydra, and you let the two rivers clean out Augeias' stables for you.' Heracles sighed.

Then Eurystheus ordered Heracles to pick him three golden apples from Hera's secret garden as his eleventh task.

'No one knows the way,' he grinned, 'except one person. And I'm not telling you who it is, so there.'

Luckily, Heracles already knew that the only person who could tell him how to get to Hera's garden was

Nereus, the Old Man of the Sea. After a long journey, he tiptoed up to the mouth of the river Po, where Nereus was taking a nap among the seaweed.

'Got you!' he cried, seizing the god in his strong arms. Nereus woke up with a jump and turned into a hissing snake. Then he turned quickly into a lion, a tiny mouse, a worm, a speck of dust and a raging fire. But Heracles held on, never letting go, and finally Nereus turned back into himself.

'What do *you* want?' he asked grumpily. Heracles told him. 'Ho!' said Nereus. 'You want to be careful picking those apples. Only gods can go into that garden. Atlas lives round there – why don't you ask him to help?' Then he gave Heracles directions and went back to his seaweed bed. 'And don't come disturbing me again, or I'll turn *you* into something!' he snarled as he closed his eyes.

Heracles took six months to reach Hera's garden, and he had many adventures getting there. On the way, he passed Prometheus, still chained to his crag in the Caucasus, and still having his liver torn out by the giant eagle every morning. When Heracles heard his groans, he went to visit him.

'Poor old chap,' he said sympathetically. 'How long is it that you've been here?'

'Thirty thousand years,' moaned Prometheus. Heracles took aim at the eagle and shot it dead, then he took his knobbly club, and started to bash and bang at Prometheus's chains.

'It's far too long,' said Heracles. 'I'm sure Zeus has forgiven you by now.' And he was quite right, Zeus had, because Prometheus had given him some very good advice over the years. But he commanded that Prometheus should always wear a chain set with stones from his mountain, so that he would never forget his crime.

When Heracles reached Hera's garden in the farthest west, he found it was surrounded by a high wall. He looked over the top, and there was a beautiful tree, with shining golden apples dangling from its branches in the light of the setting sun. Three nymphs in gauzy dresses were dancing round the tree, watched by an enormous dragon with a hundred heads, which had been set to guard the tree by Hera when her other monster, Argos, had been killed by Hermes.

As Heracles turned to go and find Atlas to help him, he saw a giant hand propping up the sky, just where it curved away on the horizon. When Heracles got nearer, he found Atlas holding up the whole heavens on his shoulders.

'Looks heavy,' he said. Atlas nodded, and the sky spilled a few stars.

'It is,' he grunted. 'Perhaps you'd like to have a go. You look a strong man, and I could do with a rest.' Heracles nodded.

'I'll do it if you go and pick me three of those golden apples over there,' he agreed. But Atlas looked worried.

'Is that dreadful dragon, Ladon, still there?' he asked. Heracles nodded again. 'Well, I won't do it unless you kill him for me. Those hundred heads give me the creeps.'

So Heracles crept back to the garden and shot Ladon in the heart with one of his deadly poisoned arrows. The dragon died so quietly that the nymphs didn't even notice.

Heracles swapped places with Atlas, who soon returned with the golden apples.

'You look very comfortable,' said Atlas, who was enjoying his freedom. 'Tell you what! I'll take the apples to King Eurystheus and you stay here for a bit.' A crafty gleam came into his eye. 'I promise to come back as soon as I've delivered them!' Heracles could see that Atlas was lying, so he thought he would play a trick on him. The sky was getting very heavy, and he couldn't possibly hold it up for another minute.

'I'll need a pad for my shoulders, then,' Heracles said quickly. 'Just hold the sky up a second while I run and get one.' Atlas put the apples on the ground and shouldered his burden once more. 'Sorry, Atlas,' said Heracles. 'But I really have to go now!' And picking up the apples, he ran off as fast as he could, with Atlas's roars ringing in his ears.

Eurystheus was amazed when he saw the golden apples.

'I can't keep them here,' he blustered. 'Take them away – they're terribly dangerous!' So Heracles went to find Athene, who took the apples back to Hera's garden and hung them on the tree again. And there

they hang to this day, sparkling in the sunset light as the three nymphs dance and play around them.

～ 46 ～

THE QUEEN'S BELT

King Eurystheus had a daughter called Admete. She was a small, scrawny, scrunched-up sort of girl with a shrill voice and a terrible temper. She was also badly spoilt, and her father gave her whatever she wanted. One day she came to see her father, just as he was climbing out of his bronze jar.

'I want a present,' she said rudely. 'And I want that stupid Heracles to get it for me.' King Eurystheus smiled at her lovingly.

'And what would my sweet girl like?' he asked.

'That Amazon Queen, Hippolyta. She's got a magic girdle that helps her fight. I want that so I can fight all the horrid people in this palace who laugh at me behind my back.'

King Eurystheus summoned Heracles at once, and told him what his next task was to be. Heracles couldn't help smiling behind his hand. The thought of scrawny little Admete fighting anyone was funny. But he had to do as Eurystheus wanted, so off he set for the river Thermodon, where the Amazons lived.

The Amazons were fierce women warriors who liked nothing better than a good fight. So Heracles thought he had better take all his weapons, just in case they were too strong for him. But when he landed his boat, a huge woman came running to greet him.

'Hail, Heracles the Hero!' she said. 'We have heard of your great deeds, and our queen would like to invite you to a feast in your honour.' Heracles was very surprised, but he went with the woman to the palace to meet Queen Hippolyta.

When Queen Hippolyta saw Heracles she was impressed with his size and strength. He told her all about his task, and she kindly agreed to give him her girdle as a present. Now the goddess Hera had disguised herself as one of the Amazons so that she could spy on Heracles, and when she learned of Queen Hippolyta's gift, she was disgusted.

'So Heracles thinks this is an easy task,' she spat. 'We'll just see about that!' And off she went to spread terrible rumours that Heracles was going to kidnap Hippolyta and carry her off. This made the other Amazons very angry indeed.

As Queen Hippolyta strode down to the shore the morning after the feast to give Heracles her girdle, the Amazons mounted their horses and charged up behind her, shooting arrows as they galloped. Heracles leapt at poor Hippolyta, seized her by the hair and tore the girdle out of her hand. Then he fought his way through the whole army of Amazons to get back to his boat, leapt aboard and set sail at once. As soon as he got back to Tiryns, he handed the girdle over to Eurystheus, who ran to find his daughter.

'Here you are, my dearest,' he said. But Admete just snatched the girdle without a word of thanks and stalked off to find someone to fight.

~ 47 ~

THE SWAMP MONSTER

For hundreds of years Hera had been protecting a dreadful monster. She thought it would be useful to have a pet monster, in case she needed it to kill someone. So when Eurystheus was thinking up another task for Heracles, she flew down from Olympus to tell him about her Hydra, hoping that it would kill Heracles with its venomous breath.

Now the Hydra lived in a sludgy, squelchy swamp just outside the city of Lerna. It had its lair underneath a tall plane tree right in the middle, where it writhed and wriggled in and out of the filthy water, hissing and spitting horribly smelly poison from its nine snaky heads. One of its heads had a large lump of gold set into it, and it was this head which was the most dangerous, because it could never die.

When Heracles was told about this task, he was in despair.

'How ever shall I kill it?' he asked his friend Iolaus. Iolaus didn't know, but the goddess Athene did, and as Heracles and Iolaus arrived at Lerna, she appeared beside them in their chariot.

'You'll never do this without some help,' she said, 'and

as Hera is helping Eurystheus, I don't see why I shouldn't help you. Now, this is what you have to do.'

Heracles followed Athene's advice exactly. He fired burning arrows at the monster to make it come out, and then held his breath while he tried to strangle it. But the monster tripped him up with its scaly tail, and although he kept cutting its heads off with his sword, more and more kept growing. Then Hera sent a huge crab to help the Hydra, and it nipped Heracles' toes till he shrieked and stamped on its shell, crushing it to death.

Iolaus saw that his friend was in trouble, so he set some branches on fire, and rushed in and burnt the stumps where Heracles had cut the Hydra's heads off. This stopped the new ones growing, and finally Heracles was able to cut the last golden head off. He carried it to the shore, and buried it, still hissing, under a great stone. Then he dipped his arrows in the Hydra's poison, making them so dangerous that the slightest wound from one would kill any living thing.

Because Iolaus had helped Heracles in his task, Eurystheus said it didn't count, and so he made Heracles do an extra task as a punishment later on. Hera was furious that her monstrous pet was dead, and it made her hate Heracles more than ever. She took the crab that had helped the Hydra, and placed it among the stars, where it hangs to this very day, nipping at the heels of any who cross its path in the sky.

~ 48 ~

BRONZE FEATHERS

After Heracles had caught the Hind of Ceryneia, King
Eurystheus couldn't think of anything
dangerous enough for him to do.
Then a messenger came from
the people of a village called
Stymphalus, to say that
they had been invaded by a
flock of dreadful birds,
which had flown down
from the north, and had
settled in the nearby marsh.
They had sharp feathers of
bronze which they plucked out
and threw at people, wounding them terribly.

'Go and get me some of those bronze feathers
immediately. They'll make a nice crown for me to wear
at the next feast,' ordered Eurystheus, who was vain as
well as cowardly. 'You can drive the birds away for the
villagers as well.'

Heracles arrived in Stymphalus at dawn. The villagers
took him to the marsh, where the birds were all roosting
in a huge flock in the very middle. As the sun rose, it

flashed off their bright feathers, and all the villagers ran away in terror. Heracles started to shoot his arrows at the birds, but they were too far away, and the arrows fell uselessly on the boggy ground.

'Looks like you need some help again, my friend,' said a voice beside him. When Heracles turned round, there was Athene, standing laughing at him and holding a great big rattle which Hephaestus the blacksmith god had made for her.

'This will make enough noise to scare those birds away forever, and you can pick up some feathers for that stupid Eurystheus when they've gone. If you tread carefully you won't sink much in the marsh, and you can collect your precious arrows at the same time.'

Heracles thanked Athene, and blocked up his ears with wax to shut out the noise. Then he started to swing the rattle. *Whirr-a-whirrrr-a-whirrrr-a-wheeee* it went, and the birds rose straight into the air, screeching with terror, and flew off. As they flew, their feathers cascaded down in showers, and the ground glittered as if it was covered with bronze-coloured snow. Heracles picked the feathers up one by one, careful not to cut his fingers on the sharp edges, and put them into a stout sack.

When he got back to Tiryns, he tipped the sack out at Eurystheus's feet.

'Ooh! Lovely!' squealed Eurystheus, grabbing at the feathers as they fell. But he was soon sorry for his greed as he dabbed at his cut and bleeding fingers.

As for the Stymphalian Birds, they never stopped flying till they reached the Isle of Ares in the Black Sea. And there they lived in peace until a ship full of heroes landed there and chased them away, and they were never heard of again.

~ 49 ~

THE GUARDIAN OF
THE UNDERWORLD

Heracles' last task was his most difficult yet.

'Go and fetch me the fearsome dog Cerberus, who guards the gates of Tartarus,' squeaked Eurystheus from the safety of his bronze jar. He knew Heracles wouldn't be very pleased.

'Very well, you wretched little man,' growled Heracles. 'But don't blame me if you're so scared when you see him that you don't come out from that jar for a whole *year*!'

The entrance to the Underworld was very hard to find, and Heracles spent a long time looking for it. He found it at last, but he was in a terrible temper as he

climbed down the dark dark passages to Hades' kingdom. When he reached the river Styx, he aimed an arrow at the old boatman, Charon.

'Take me across, or else,' he shouted, and as he stepped into the wobbly boat, Charon started rowing as fast as he could. The ghosts on the far side twittered and rustled as he brushed through them, and although he stopped to talk to one or two old friends, Heracles was still in a bad mood. Hades himself trembled at the look on Heracles' face when he marched up to the outer gates of the palace.

'Give me that dog,' Heracles demanded, pointing at the horrid three-headed dog growling by the gate. Its heads and back were covered with a mane of writhing snakes, its teeth were as long as spears and it had a lashing serpent's tail. Its great round eyes were as big as cartwheels, and redder than rubies.

Hades bowed and rubbed his hands together.

'Take him with pleasure,' he said. 'But you mustn't use your arrows or club.'

'Fine!' said Heracles grimly, and he put on the armour he had made from the skin of the Nemean lion. Then he started to wrestle with Cerberus. What a great fight it was. Cerberus bit with all three mouths, and his snake mane hissed and spat, but Heracles hung on and on and on until Cerberus gave up and lay down, all four paws pointing to the dark sky above. Heracles dragged him up to earth, and threw him out of the door of the Underworld into the light of day. Cerberus whimpered as the bright sunshine hit his eyes, and then he started to bark. Great drops of slobber flew from his jaws, and as they landed on the fields, they turned into the poisonous yellow flowers we call aconites.

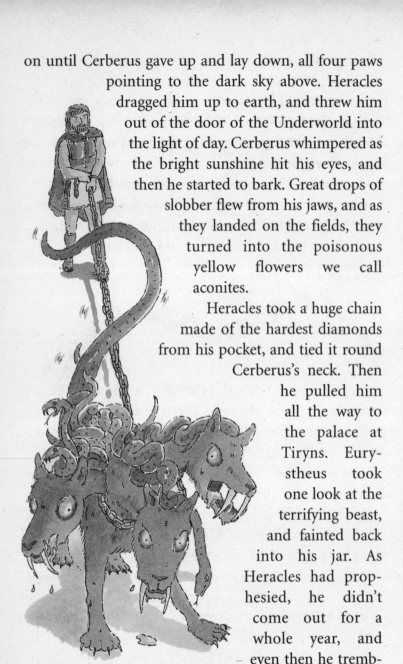

Heracles took a huge chain made of the hardest diamonds from his pocket, and tied it round Cerberus's neck. Then he pulled him all the way to the palace at Tiryns. Eurystheus took one look at the terrifying beast, and fainted back into his jar. As Heracles had prophesied, he didn't come out for a whole year, and even then he trembled so much that he couldn't eat more than a mouthful at a time.

Heracles didn't know what to do with Cerberus, so he took him back to Tartarus and gave him back to Hades. His twelve tasks were finished and he was a free man at last. Zeus was proud of his fine son, and vowed that one day he should come and live on Olympus. But Heracles travelled round Greece for many more years before that happened, performing greater and greater deeds until there was no one in the whole world who had not heard of Heracles the Hero.

~ 50 ~

THE POISONED ROBE

The river-god Achelous was in love with Deianeira, the beautiful daughter of King Oeneus of Calydon. He had the monstrous head of a bull, with a shaggy wet beard hanging down from his chin, and Deianeira hated him. At that time the hero Heracles was travelling through Calydon, and when he saw Deianeira he knew at once that he wanted to marry her. She was so relieved to have another suitor that she said yes to Heracles immediately, but when Achelous heard that she was going to marry someone else he roared with rage.

'Show me this hero,' he shouted. 'Let him fight me if he wants to marry you!'

Now Heracles knew all about fighting monsters, and he soon defeated Achelous, who slunk away in shame to a cave made of willow branches. Heracles and Deianeira were soon married, and lived very happily until one day they had to go on a long journey to a place called

Trachis. After a while they came to a wide river.

'Oh please don't make me cross it,' cried Deianeira. 'Achelous might come up out of the water and carry me off.' Heracles tried to reassure her, jumping across and back in two great leaps to show her that there was no danger. But still she wouldn't cross. Just then an evil centaur called Nessus came running up.

'I will carry you across, pretty lady. You will be quite safe with me!' Deianeira was pleased, but as soon as Nessus had carried her across the river, he galloped away from Heracles, with Deianeira clinging to his back.

'Help me, Heracles,' she cried, so Heracles strung one of his magic arrows and shot Nessus through the chest.

'Take my magic blood, Deianeira,' whispered the wicked centaur, as he lay dying. 'And if you ever doubt your husband, dip his tunic in it and then he will stay faithful to you and love you forever.' Deianeira did as he said, and caught the precious blood in a little bottle.

Heracles and Deianeira arrived at the end of their journey, and settled comfortably into the palace at

Trachis. But one day Deianeira caught Heracles looking at one of her ladies in waiting, and she became very jealous. That night she dipped Heracles' best tunic in the centaur's blood, and put it out for him to wear the next morning.

As soon as Heracles put the tunic on he began to gasp with pain. Terrible blisters erupted all over his body, and his very bones felt as if they were on fire. Deianeira began to shriek and cry. She had not known that Nessus's blood was poisonous to mortals, and that this was his revenge on Heracles for killing him.

Heracles was in such pain that he tried to rip off the tunic, but it was stuck to his body. He ran out of the palace and plunged into the nearest stream, but it was no good, the waters just bubbled and boiled with the heat. Heracles knew it was time for him to die, and he asked his friends to build a pyre of oak and olive branches. As soon as it was ready, he spread his lion skin on top of it and lay down, after giving his bow and arrows to his friend Philoctetes. Then Zeus sent down a bright bolt of lightning, and Heracles rose up to Olympus on a shining jet of thunder and flame. There Heracles shed his mortal skin, and the gods welcomed him with seven days of feasting and laughter for the bravest hero ever known in heaven or on earth.